S0-EFO-213

Praise for Ciar Cullen's Mayan Nights

From Fallen Angel Reviews--5 Angels! "Kudos to Ms. Cullen. She really knows how to portray the heroine as strong, yet at the same time vulnerable. Tamara Martin is a woman who knows what she wants, not only in her professional life, but in her sexual life as well. And she is not afraid to chase after either one to obtain them. You find yourself enchanted with the Mayan jungle and yet cursing the heat at the same time. Ms. Cullen has a wonderful talent for pulling the reader into the story and experiencing everything along with the characters. Praise for her imagination and colorful imagery into Mayan Nights."

From a Romance Review "The humorous war of words and sizzling, sexual escapades of Tam and Sinjin make Mayan Nights a fast-paced novel. Lost among the pages of the seductive Yucatan jungle, you reach the last chapter long before you know it! With the broad scope of Ciar Cullen's storytelling, she weaves a magical tale of passion, danger, mystery and love that transcends time, a love that ultimately conquers all. Mayan Nights is a shelf keeper and I am eagerly awaiting whatever Ms. Cullen has in store for the sequel!"

From Romance Junkies: "MAYAN NIGHTS is an engrossing, thrill ride of a book with enough heat to put even the Mexican jungle to shame. Ciar Cullen has crafted a passionate tale with a bit of a mystery and a paranormal twist. The characters in this book are larger than life and as for the love scenes, all I can say is Wow! Ms Cullen has written some thrilling, steamy sex scenes that will leave you panting."

From Pink Posse: A 5 Pink Hats Off Salute to Ciar Cullen. I have three words that sum up, "Mayan Nights"... HOT, HOT, HOT! This story has exquisite attention to detail, intelligent characters and literally oozes with sensuality. Ciar Cullen's research & knowledge of location, with a bit of archaeology thrown in plus action/adventure, is a very clever mix of old vs. new vs. old. If you like your protagonists smart, your locations tropical & your sex steamy you must read this tale! This is one sultry read. I look forward to being transported by Ms Cullen on any of her further adventures."

From Euro-Reviews: Ciar Cullen is a true story teller which is very evident in Mayan Nights. "Once upon a time, there was a lovely young woman," starts this story as told by Shield Jaguar. In between that and the happily ever after is a love story rich in development with likable characters, some little spooky curse issues, hot steamy sex and a bad guy which all leads to a very satisfying ending. Tam Martin is a wonderfully strong heroine who goes after what she wants and uses her brain in every instance. With a wonderful twist to the stereo type, the hero, SinJin, has a painful personal past and HIS emotions get in the way and cloud his judgment throughout the book creating problems, discord and almost disaster. He also happens to like his woman a bit forceful in the bedroom.

5 Stars from eCataromance! "Mayan Nights is stunning, searing and hysterically funny! Ciar Cullen writes a dazzling narrative of love and passion that affects everything, including time itself!"

Meet Ciar Cullen

Ciar Cullen grew up in Baltimore, Maryland--Charm City--and has lived a charmed life. She worked for a decade as an archaeologist, summering on digs in Greece. Ciar has a strong interest in history of all periods. She worked for years in academic nonfiction publishing and is currently a bureaucrat at a prominent college. Ciar took up writing in 2004 to scratch an itch brought on by years of reading fantasy and romance fiction. She submitted her first book on a whim, and hasn't turned back. Her favorite authors are Terry Pratchett, Mark Twain, and Roger Zelazny. Ciar lives in New Jersey with her wonderful husband and magical cat.

You can learn more about her at www.ciarcullen.com.

What's coming next

Lords of Ch'i - September 2006
The Princes of Anfall - December 2006
The Serpent House – March 2007
Unholy Vows – June 2007
Dark Prince of Anfall – September 2007
The Ghosts of Key West – December 2007

Mayan Nights

By Ciar Cullen

A Samhain Publishing, Ltd. publication

Samhain Publishing, Ltd.
PO Box 2206
Stow OH 44224

Mayan Nights
Copyright © 2006 by Ciar Cullen
Cover by Scott Carpenter
Print ISBN: 1-59998-207-2
Digital ISBN: 1-59998-013-4
www.samhainpublishing.com

This book is a work of fiction. The names, characters, places, and incidents
are products of the writer's imagination or have been used fictitiously and are
not to be construed as real. Any resemblance to persons, living or dead, actual
events, locale or organizations is entirely coincidental.

All Rights Are Reserved. No part of this book may be used or reproduced in
any manner whatsoever without written permission, except in the case of brief
quotations embodied in critical articles and reviews.

First Samhain Publishing, Ltd. electronic publication: March 2006
This title has been previously published.

Mayan Nights

By Ciar Cullen

Acknowlegements

Warm thanks to the staff of Samhain Publishing, and to Bruce, for his unwavering support and love.

Prologue

"Can't sleep, dear?"

Shield Jaguar's young wife shook her head and snuggled closer, running her fingers through his long hair, playing with the feathers braided into his royal topknot. She sighed in pleasure as he rubbed her back. Her huge brown eyes pleaded for his attention, tugging at his heart. Lady A'ok feared the night, the death of the Sun. For weeks, Shield Jaguar had humored his new consort, giving her attention as if she were the one who ruled Pacal herself.

"I neglect my duties, attending to your insatiable need for attention and pleasure. The priests mutter amongst themselves, but loud enough that I might hear. If you tell anyone how you have turned me into a simpering lovesick boy, I'll order your execution."

"You are a boy."

He growled in mock anger. The residents of Pacal had taken to affectionately calling him the 'Boy King', their youngest leader ever at twenty. Certainly, his consort looked far younger than her eighteen years, and she always laughed at the jokes at her expense.

"I meant only that you are young to rule such a proud people and magnificent city!" A'ok winked, poking her tongue in her cheek. Shield Jaguar loved the dimples that came to life in her face when she teased, which was often.

"You are younger still, to rule alongside me. Perhaps I needed a wiser, more mature consort..."

She ignored his taunt and ran her hand along his arm.

"Are you really lovesick? How does it feel? Tell me what you like about me?" Her precious smile warmed his heart and his cock, and for the hundredth time, he thanked all the gods for their wisdom in choosing this girl.

"No. I have told you enough. It is your turn to lavish me with praise!"

Shield Jaguar laughed as A'ok wrinkled her nose in disappointment. He clutched at her perfect soft hips, moving lower to squeeze her wonderful buttocks. Shield Jaguar held her gaze steadily with the dark look he knew excited her, as he unfastened her feathered skirt and slid his fingers down her stomach to toy with the nest of delicate black hair, lower to toy with the moist folds he craved. She squirmed and moaned under his touch.

"Tell me a story." A'ok caressed his chest, slowly moving her hand down his ribcage, and lower, to her prize. He moaned in pleasure, never tiring of her talented hands. She ran her thumb over the head of his cock and pulled teasingly, licking her full lips in glee.

"So subtle, my dear."

"It works."

"In more ways than one. I believe Lady A'ok means to turn her king into her sexual slave."

"I believe the King of Pacal is very wise, indeed, despite his youth."

"You are truly happy with this union?" Shield Jaguar winced at his own weakness, the need to hear it again. All the women of Pacal wanted him, and yet, this one woman's desire was paramount.

"I live to serve my King." She began a steady stroke of his cock as she nibbled playfully on his nipples.

Shield Jaguar watched her in awe. How did her beauty grow daily? Her skills did as well, for in seconds, fire coursed to his cock and he became breathless. Still, he wanted her words as much as her body.

She adores you; can't you see it in her eyes? She must tell you, though—do not be the first to utter the words. It does not become the ruler of Pacal to beg for love.

A'ok worked her way down his torso, teasing with her tongue until she captured the head of his cock between her lips. Staring up at him, she worked him deep into her throat. Her moans tortured him with pleasure; he reached out to hold her head and caress her silken hair as she began a rhythmic sucking.

Shield Jaguar fought to hold her gaze, the first hint of release filling him to bursting. His need built with the strokes of her tongue and her moans of appreciation, but he pushed her head away. Not like this, not tonight. Tonight he would make her wild for him, ensure she fell deeper, further, into the depths of passion, so far that she would never want another, never even look at another.

Before the night is over, she will tell you she loves you. She will be your slave, and if the gods approve, she will become the mother of a King.

"What kind of story would you like tonight, A'ok?"

"I can listen and suck on you at the same time. I am quite talented that way. Oh, I see you intend to be difficult."

"I, however, cannot tell a story with your beautiful lips driving me into oblivion. I would like to extend the evening a bit." Shield Jaguar gestured for her to lie next to him and slid his palm along her breast, teasing the dark hard nipple between his fingers.

"Ah, Lord, you have the hands of the gods."

"I am a god." He leaned in and suckled at her breast, caressing the other with his hand. "I asked you a question, woman. The King is not to be ignored."

"Oh...How am I to speak? Tell me a story of the ones who come after us—a tale with some good parts. Make them really in love, insane for one another, mad with lust, lots of sex! The kind with binding and playful torture, too! Make sure he touches himself, you know how I love that!"

"I have never known a woman to enjoy such torrid talk. My words seem to please you as much as my hands, my lips, my essence releasing inside you."

"Your stories are wonderful. I have never known a man with such an imagination. It's one of the reasons I..."

"Yes?" Shield Jaguar held his breath, relieved the moment was at hand.

"One of the reasons I enjoy our nights together so much. Not the greatest reason." She pulled his head back to her breast and clutched at his hair. "Please?"

He sat up and rubbed his chin, as if he were considering her request, as if this were a new game. Perhaps it was time to make her understand what it was to be the Jaguar King. To become the god of all the people, the most powerful creature of El Mundo Maya, to assume the immortal form. A'ok did not yet understand his power, his ability to look through time to eternity, to a place where the Sun rose and fell in days that each seemed to last a thousand years. His family's priests wisely guarded the royal secrets, and none but he and his mother and brothers endured the rituals that provided the deep knowing, the connection to the Mayan cosmos. A'ok might never understand his world, but he wanted her love so badly, wanted her to know him completely.

"Very well, a story about the future. Let's see... Ah, I have just the one. It involves a very special man, you will fall in love with him, I am certain of it. This man will be important to my destiny, as you shall see. All right, as they say in the days far along the wheel of the calendar, "Once upon a time, there was a lovely young woman..."

Chapter One

"St. John Twaine? The Ivy League Beast? You *cannot* be serious! He's wiped out *at least* four researchers in the last two years. You didn't tell me you were joining *him*."

Tam ignored Jack's nervous pacing and tried to block out his arguments as she packed.

"Look, I need this. He's sitting on the most exciting Mayan finds in decades. If I can get a piece of this publication, I'm set. My phone isn't exactly ringing off the hook with other offers."

"He *shot at me!* Are you listening? The man is a lunatic. Too much time in the Mexican sun, too much tequila, and the rumor is that he really lost it after his wife died." Jack poked a finger at her. "It's not exactly clear *how* she died. What do you say about that?"

"Bullshit, that's what I say. He's a tenured Princeton professor—a brilliant one—and he didn't get that far on tequila and wife-mutilation. You read too many romances. Do most gay men read romances? I think that's fascinating. Really. Do you picture that you're the woman? Of course, you'd have to."

"Don't try to distract me with insults. Explain why Twaine's stayed in the field for four years? Every

14

archaeologist I know comes back after the season to a nice little house near the college, a respectable little wife, and a sensible Volvo."

"So he's an eccentric academician. Remember, I can handle eccentric academicians. I'm a Martin."

"Your family isn't this weird, trust me. It's not just him, there's the site. Of course, I wasn't at Pacal for more than an hour or so, *before he shot at me*, but something about the place really creeped me out."

"Come on, the Pacal curse? Don't disturb the tombs of the dead? You probably believe in the curse of King Tut's tomb too? Puh-lease."

"You'll see. I'll pick you up at the airport—let's say in a week or so. We'll have dinner, and you can tell me all about your one fantastic night in Cozmano. Just don't piss him off and get shot."

"Very funny. Can you at least drive me to the airport without nagging?"

Jack sighed in resignation and nodded.

"Tam, one more thing."

"Hmm?" She sorted through the mound of clothes on her bed, quickly pulling out summer garb for the jungle and a few classier designer items to impress the great Professor.

"I'm not an expert on these things, but I imagine most women might think Twaine's attractive in some perverse way. Despite the guns."

Tam snorted. "Well, I suppose you would know."

"He's not my type. My gay-dar works perfectly, thank you very much. Twaine's as straight as they come, damn it."

"Well, he certainly won't be my type." *He probably wears a tweed jacket to dinner. No doubt smokes a pipe.* Of course, Twaine was young by Princeton standards. Still, she hadn't seen a sexy professor on campus in the five years it had taken to get her doctorate.

"Why are we talking about Twaine's sex appeal, anyway? I'd rather screw one of the handsome local lads, if it comes to that, and it won't! Every time I get near you I end up talking about sex."

Jack arched a brow at her and she threw a bra at him. "I think it's called nymphomania. Simply put, you're a 'ho'."

"So are you."

"That's why we get along. We can talk about big cocks together."

"You're vulgar, really Jack." Tam laughed at Jack's leer. "Are you sure, absolutely, positively sure?"

"Not *that* again. It's not reversible, Tam. But if I ever feel the urge to do a woman, you'll be the first to know. You really can't imagine that a man wouldn't want you, can you? God, it must be rough to be you."

If you only knew, my friend. Tam took a long look at Jack, wondering if he really understood how special he was, how she longed for a man like him...with one difference. He really was the perfect guy; incredibly handsome, built, great taste in clothes, and could he *cook.* Most of all, he respected her, her work, her devotion to her career, her independence.

"Oh, most guys want me for at least one night, until they find out I'm more intelligent than they are."

"Come on, baby, you're the one who dumps them."

"Okay, so maybe I like my men smart. Sue me."

"Hmm, Twaine's actually pretty smart. Brilliant, in fact. Careful, Tam, I'm serious."

"But does he have a big cock?"

"Charming. Do send me a postcard and let me know. On a serious note, I'll point out that your plane takes off in three hours, and it takes an hour these days to clear customs out of Philly."

Tam hugged Jack tightly. "I'll miss you, baby. I wish you could come with."

"I had my fill of Pacal, and Twaine. Tam?"

"Hmm?"

"I don't think you're going to need those heels and stockings."

"You never know. He's upper crust, old money, and first impressions are very important. I'm taking the Indiana Jones gear, too, don't worry."

"Me, worry?"

Sweat drenched every inch of her. Her smart linen suit looked like a crumpled dishrag. Her soaked hair hung limply. Tam wiped off the last remaining streaks of makeup and smashed a mosquito on her arm, where it left a drop of her blood. It was the bus ride from hell.

"Shoo." A chicken pecked at her Prada shoes while its foul-smelling owner snored across the aisle.

Another pothole the size of a moon crater, another wind in the road, another lurch to a sudden stop, and Tam thought she would lose her breakfast. Photos of half-naked women hung next to rosaries from the driver's rearview mirror. Everything about the last two hours infuriated her.

Diesel fumes spewed out in huge clouds as the death-trap rolled to a halt.

"Cozmano," the fat greasy driver growled, gesturing slightly with his head as he straightened his pornographic photo collection and rosary beads.

"Sorry? *Por favor?*" It couldn't be. There was nothing more than a dirt path and a big rock with an arrow painted on it.

"Cozmano." He gestured emphatically and muttered something obscene. "Professor Sin." He pointed again.

Professor Sin?

A local helped her drag her suitcase off the bus. "Señorita, I am Orlando. If you come for Señor Twaine, we will meet again. I work at his ruins."

"Oh! I'm very pleased to meet you, Orlando! My name is Tam."

Orlando eyed her quickly from head to toe and tipped his hat. "Señorita, I mean no offense, but how well do you know the Professor?"

"I've never met the man."

"He does not take well to females."

"Excuse me?"

"My English, my meaning maybe, is not so clear. There has never been a female on the site. He prefers the men, you understand? Not in the kitchen or the bedroom, no! But at the site, you see? He says they cannot pull the weight. I heard him talk of the new assistant, but I think he expects someone...else. Does he know you're a woman?"

Tam's annoyance grew by the second. Ridiculous! More than half the archaeological community was female. What century spawned this asshole Twaine? *He must have known Princeton was sending a woman. But they might have only mentioned her last name. How could it possibly matter to him?*

The driver called Orlando back to his seat, and Tam watched the bus pull away in a cloud of diesel fumes, a sinking feeling in the pit of her stomach.

"Suck it up, Tam. This is your big break. Doesn't matter what the great professor thinks, you're going to set the world on fire."

She took in a deep breath and started up the steep, stony road. After turning her ankle twice in the deep tire ruts, she pulled her shoes off and ducked behind a bush to take off her pantyhose. The searing midday sun scorched her face, leaving her parched and cursing Twaine for not sending a car to the airport.

Making me hike up this damned road in the heat. At least a hundred degrees. So the asshole doesn't like women on the site, eh? We'll see about that. Can't pull their weight! I can read Mayan glyphs with my eyes closed, buddy, can you?

By the time she reached the top of the road, Tam's mind reeled in fury, her head pounded, her feet bled from sharp rocks lodged in the parched soil, and her arms and legs ached and felt heavy as lead. Immense relief swept through her when she finally caught sight of the hacienda nestled in the shade of lush greenery. The stately old building looked like paradise.

Come on, Martin, you can do this. Only a few hundred yards. At least the Professor was close by now and would help her. Surely this Orlando fellow was wrong. St. John Twaine would welcome her graciously, make this hellish day worth it. Offer her iced tea, be very apologetic about not being able to pick her up himself. *SinJin,* she practiced the Brit pronunciation several times, trying to ensure it would sound natural when she greeted him. No doubt, the Professor was having a very civilized lunch at this hour, or perhaps making notes of the morning's excavations. Maybe he had grown tired at the site and was enjoying a siesta.

Tam pulled off her dusty sunglasses to get a better view of a man who had wandered onto the broad porch of the hacienda. He was tall, well over six feet. She squinted and covered a few more yards. One of the workers? Definitely not Mexican, definitely not shy. His worn fatigue shorts hung so low that Tam could make out the cords of muscles hugging his hips, pointing downwards towards what looked like a promising package beneath the thin fabric. He certainly wasn't dressed for visitors.

"How about a little help here, Señor?"

He watched her calmly as he sipped an amber-colored liquid from a smeared glass. *Liquor?* The thought of drinking hard alcohol in the scorching midday sun made Tam's stomach roll. She dropped the suitcase into the dust along with her jacket and hobbled up to the house. He looked amused at her struggle, and fury overtook her again. *Didn't it just figure? The asshole had to be drop-dead gorgeous.* He was probably only thirty-four or so, but he looked a bit older, tanned deeply by the Mexican sun, a bit tired looking, with a hint of dark circles under his eyes. *A drunk?* His dark brown hair hadn't been cut in months hanging well past his ears in sun-streaked waves. His eyes were chocolate brown pools that turned to dark slits as he squinted against the sun to stare her down.

Maybe he's the professor's errant son. No, too old. Must be his brother, his drunken brother.

Tam felt his close examination as his gaze swept up her legs to her chest, where it lingered. She looked down to see her lacy white camisole, transparent with sweat.

"Never seen breasts before, Señor? Did you get a good look? Want me to strip down in exchange for some water? How about a lap dance?"

He laughed lightly and leaned patiently against a porch column.

"I seem to have stumbled onto the set of *Survivor*. You want me to get kicked off the island, is that it?"

"Are you always in such a good mood, or is this just my lucky day?" His mild accent threw her. Tam cursed to herself. As if looking like a movie star wasn't enough, he had to have that sexy accent. *Here's trouble, Tam. He's a bad boy—drinking in the middle of the day, nasty, rude, dark and brooding, a breast man—everything you love in a guy. Steer clear.*

"All right. Since you won't help me, perhaps you can tell me where I can find Professor Twaine?"

"Gone." He took a sip from his glass as he continued to stare her down in challenge.

"Gone? What do you mean? Isn't this his house? I'm Doctor Tamara Martin, his new assistant."

"Gone out into the field, *Doctor* Martin. Won't be back for hours."

"Well, can you help me? As I said, I'm his new assistant from Princeton and I..." Tam thought for a second an earthquake was hitting the Mayan Riviera, then realized the ground wasn't moving. Her last thought before passing out was that Twaine would think she was soft.

"Oh, for chrissakes."

SinJin saw her sway and before he could reach her, she collapsed in a heap on the ground. So much for the white suit. Then he saw her feet, bleeding from a hundred cuts. How the hell had she walked up the road like that? Well, he'd get her out of the sun, give her some water, and give her a lift into town. Then call Princeton and ball them out for sending a girl to do a man's job. What kind of babies were they putting through the department these days? They would fucking hear about this one. He could take his research to Harvard or Yale, and it was time to let them know it. Typical. His asshole colleagues knew how to keep alumni dollars rolling in and how to preach old-school archaeology to clueless kids, but they couldn't find him a competent assistant.

SinJin glanced down at the flushed cheeks of the young lady he held in his arms. She seemed bright enough, at least she had a personality and a flair for language.

But what kind of imbecile wears a suit into the Yucatan jungle, in the middle of August?

SinJin looked around for his housekeeper. "Rosa!"

The matron waddled onto the porch, squealing in horror at the sight of the unconscious woman. SinJin carried her into his room and laid her gently on his bed. He felt her head and groaned. *This could actually be serious.*

"Rosa, give her water, a little at a time. She's badly dehydrated. Please wash her down with cool water and see to her feet. She needs antibacterial cream."

Rosa caught her breath at the sight of the girl's bloodied soles. "Mother of God, who is she? What happened to her?"

"Princeton sent her. I'm putting her on the first plane back to New Jersey tomorrow."

"Professor SinJin, she cannot travel for a few days."

"We'll see."

SinJin spent the evening on the porch, sipping wine and writing in his notebook, toying with the idea of calling Princeton and quitting outright. The girl would have to go, of course. She was probably a hack. Too good looking to be competent on the dig, to be dedicated enough to tough it out. *A shame, really, she would have been nice eye candy.*

He drifted into the twilight between waking and sleep, thinking of Shield Jaguar's tomb. Deep sleep finally pulled him away from fretting about the dig.

A lovely blonde came to him in the dark, whispering her desires as she let her dress fall to the floor. Quick hard desire filled him at the site of her bare breasts, her legs, a tiny patch of silk hugging her pussy. He reached to pull her down, dying to rip off her thong, take her onto his hard cock, find his release. She smiled slyly, pushed his hands away, and knelt beside him. She stripped off his pants and whispered into his ear, flicking her tongue inside to heat up every word.

"SinJin, I'm so wet, so hot. Don't you want to feel how wet I am? Tell me what you want. What's your fantasy, SinJin? The one you won't tell anyone."

She fondled his swollen cock and brought her wet lips onto the head, rubbing it back and forth until he moaned in blissful agony. He looked down to see her huge blue eyes gleam in pleasure as she took him deep into her throat. Moaning and fighting his release, he wondered how he could make her go on forever.

"Who are you? Tell me, please."

She smiled and tore off her thong, revealing the wet folds ready to engulf his world. Ever so slowly she lowered herself onto his cock, moaning in pleasure as she moved up and down, clenching onto his hardness to milk him dry.

"Tell me your name," he begged again, panting in pleasure. He was ready to explode when he saw a glint of moonlight against a blade. She moved the knife to his chest. He struggled, but found that his arms were bound to the bed. When he tried to scream, no sound would come from his mouth. She slowly pressed the knife into his chest, whispering her love for him.

SinJin bolted upright, soaked with sweat, heart pounding. Why the hell was he dreaming about the Princeton girl, Doctor Martin? *Get her out of here, SinJin. You don't need the distraction.*

Chapter Two

Tam woke with a pounding headache and slowly took in her surroundings, remembering she was at Hacienda Cozmano, remembered fainting onto the dirt path in front of the arrogant hunk. She reached for the bottle of water on the nightstand and sipped slowly as she tried to sit up. The room spun a bit and she lay back down.

A light breeze blew in through the window, stirring lovely sheer white curtains hand-embroidered in traditional Mayan floral designs. The room was furnished in heavy antique wooden furniture and would have looked stark were it not for the soft touches in every corner—a small vase full of wildflowers, a crocheted throw of delicate lace, a hand-carved statue of the Virgin, and an artful arrangement of candles and traditional pottery on a small low table.

The song of birds filled the air and the room grew brighter by the minute. Tam glanced at her watch and realized in shock that the streaks of light now streaming into the room signaled sunrise. She'd slept like the dead for at least fifteen hours! Low voices and the clanking of dishes from the porch outside her window stirred her nerves. What would the professor think? Intent on apologizing for being such an inconvenience, Tam sat up, working her way to the edge of the bed, fighting the cloudiness of her brain. *Get it together, Martin! You have to make a good first impression on Twaine.*

When she pushed herself to her feet, she nearly crumpled to the floor in agony and sat back down to examine her wounds. Someone had wrapped gauze bandages around her feet, now stained with the blood of what looked like dozens of small cuts. Surely that oaf hadn't been the one to treat her wounds? Who had changed her into a simple *huipile*, a Mayan cotton shift?

She listened carefully and heard the lilting tones of a woman speaking in Spanish. Hobbling painfully to the window, Tam peaked out to see the arrogant bastard sitting alone at a table, bare-chested, wolfing down eggs and toast. A rotund middle-aged Mayan woman poured a cup of coffee for him and he smiled broadly at her in appreciation. Tam nearly gasped at the change in his face, the open affection for the woman reflected in his beautiful brown eyes.

Perhaps she had caught him at a bad moment yesterday. A wave of relief swept through her. He looked reasonable enough now, and no doubt would give her the welcome she deserved, take her to Twaine.

She found her way to a small bathroom off the bedroom and pulled off her shift, anxious to clean up a bit and put on her own clothes, which were arranged neatly on a bench along one wall. After toweling down with cool water, she pulled on a sundress and took a step back to look into the small mirror hanging on the wall. The sight shocked her—she was pale as a ghost, with dark circles under her eyes.

"You'll impress Twaine all right. He'll probably send you packing."

There was no sense in putting off the inevitable, so Tam painfully pulled on flip-flops and quietly stepped onto the porch, plastering a smile on her face.

"Good morning," Tam said cheerfully.

The Mayan woman approached Tam and stood on tiptoes to feel her forehead.

"No fever, but you look unwell. Are you sure you don't want to stay in bed, miss?"

"I'm just fine, thanks."

The woman made a clucking noise to indicate she wasn't buying Tam's claim and indicated a seat at the table across from the other houseguest, who didn't acknowledge her presence.

"*Huevos?* Eggs, miss?"

"No, maybe just some toast, Señora."

"Please, call me Rosa. I am Professor Twaine's housekeeper."

"Did you dress me and take care of my feet? I really appreciate it."

"My pleasure. Now, tell me the truth, how do you feel this morning?"

"Like I was hit by a train. It's a bit of sunstroke, I guess." Tam thought the man snickered softly, but she wasn't sure. Who could be so rude as to find her condition amusing?

"Keep drinking water all day, and get lots of rest."

Rosa left Tam alone with the idiot, waiting impatiently for a greeting she suspected wouldn't come. He held up a newspaper and whistled idly as he sipped at his coffee.

"I'm Tamara Martin. You are...?"

He ignored her.

"Listen, asshole, I don't know what your problem is, but when the Professor gets back, I'm going to let him know how rude you were to me yesterday. Making me drag that bag up this road. For God's sake, put on some clothes! You're on a professional dig."

He snorted at that, drained his mug, stood, and made a sarcastic sweeping bow to Tam.

"Jackass."

"I'll be sure and let the Professor know your thoughts on my behavior and the dig's dress code."

"You're going to the site? Please tell Professor Twaine that I look forward to meeting him. My feet should be all right by tomorrow and I'll be able to contribute. You'll at least pass on that message?"

He grabbed keys from the table and ran down the stairs to the Land Rover. Tam stood and called after him, repeating her question, but he ignored her, tearing down the road in a swirl of dust.

What will he tell Twaine about me? Damn. Well, there's not much you can do 'til they pack up for the day.

Tam sipped coffee and took in the lovely grounds fronting the hacienda, no doubt an old plantation house. The structure was surely well over a hundred years, but well kept, with bright tiles and potted plants betraying a woman's touch. The enchanting ruins of a tiny Missionera chapel peaked out from the jungle's edge, and Tam hobbled painfully to explore it more closely, finding a small shrine to the Virgin against one wall—a humble altar covered with dying flowers and candle stubs.

When she returned to the porch, Rosa brought Tam's meal and refilled her coffee cup.

"Oh, Professor SinJin is already gone? I wanted to ask him about dinner!"

"Professor SinJin? What do you mean?"

"St. John. You know, it is said 'SinJin'. It is a little joke in these parts to call him Professor Sin, although that is his name really, do you see? Very funny."

"I'm sorry, Rosa. You'll have to explain something to me." *No! It wasn't possible.* "Who was that man who left in the Land Rover?"

"What do you mean, miss? Professor Twaine? Did you not come here to work with him?" Rosa giggled a bit, evidently tickled by Tam's situation.

"Oh, dear God." Tam rubbed her forehead. "Rosa, I called the Professor a jackass. And an asshole."

"I think I heard you tell him to put on some clothes too, miss?"

"Yeah, that too. Oh God."

"I think he looks pretty good undressed. I would hate to see him change that." Rosa laughed harder, clapping her hands in little gestures of glee.

"Oh, God."

Rosa continued giggling as she made her way back to the kitchen, leaving Tam alone to pick at her meal. She finally gave up on food and limped back and forth across the porch, swearing up a blue streak. *You've done it now, Martin. Nice job. You called the great SinJin Twaine a jackass.*

Rosa reemerged onto the porch, wiping her hands on her apron.

"Sit, miss, please. Your feet will open up again!"

"Sorry about the cursing, Rosa."

"I've heard cursing before, Dr. Martin. A good deal of cursing, actually. Don't be upset about calling SinJin a jackass. He hears worse, you may trust Rosa on this fact."

"I'm such a goddamned idiot. I simply cannot shut up. Ever. This was my big chance. Oh well, he won't make me limp down to the bus stop, will he? He's not that much of an asshole, right?"

"I don't think he's that much of an asshole." Rosa shook her head seriously.

Tam continued her painful pacing, and to her embarrassment, tears started to flow down her cheeks.

"Oh Doctor Martin, stop it now. This is not good for your feet. Perhaps it's for the best. Most of his assistants—actually *all* of his assistants—leave, sooner or later."

"I'm tougher than that, Rosa. I don't care about his bad attitude, and I'm a better archaeologist than anyone else Princeton's sent him. No, I fucked up royally this time."

She sank onto a porch chair and let the tears take over. Rosa sat with her and gently rubbed her back until she calmed down.

"I cry when I'm angry. Sorry."

"Don't apologize. I do the same thing."

"This place..." Tam gestured at the grounds of Cozmano. "It's perfect. I would have been happy here, I know it." Tam took in the smells, sounds, and caressing warm air and let them fill her close to tears again. A colorful bird streaked through the air and landed on a nearby branch. Its exotic cry echoed, the forlorn sound clutching at her chest.

"I guess I'll never see my jaguar."

"Your jaguar?"

"I've dreamt for years of seeing one in the wild. I planned on going south at the end of the season, maybe to the wildlife refuge." Tam shook her head in dismay and sighed. "What I wouldn't give to be at Pacal with the Professor right now, Rosa. Bad attitude and all. He is a real bear, though, isn't he?" She managed to laugh a little.

"A bear? I do not know this joke. You poor thing, perhaps he will change his mind."

"He's written me off already. Nothing will change his mind, short of a miraculous discovery of my own." *If only I had one chance to show him what I can do.*

"I don't think the Professor cares about the things you said, Dr. Martin. He's not very...sensitive about what strangers think of him."

Tam barely heard the woman, desperately searching for a way to demonstrate her skills. How could she get to the site? Impossible.

"Rosa, does the Professor work here, at the house?"

"Of course. He works all the time, as soon as he comes back from the site, sometimes into the night. Almost every day of the year, except..."

"What?"

"Never mind, I talk too much myself."

"Come on, Rosa. Help me out here. You know I probably blew my chance at this job. I'm trying to get it back. Please?"

"Miss, I never talk about SinJin, but because you're a pretty single lady...maybe you won't want to stay? He's...a little different. Sometimes the sadness comes over him. You know what I mean?"

"Grief, you mean? Because his wife died."

"Then you have heard of his loss. His wife, yes, and his baby. That's part of it."

Tam took in a breath. *Baby?*

"It was too soon, the birth, and Laura hadn't been well."

"I didn't know. How awful."

Rosa nodded. "Yes, I was with him then. Miss Laura, she was very young, and not cut out for this life, you see? Not always so kind to me." She lowered her voice. "Not so kind to him either. Do you understand my meaning? I don't think she wanted to be here. But SinJin wanted to stay, you see? Nothing could drag him from Pacal, not even the health of his wife."

Tam nodded thoughtfully. No wonder he was a bastard. His wife died in childbirth in the middle of nowhere because he insisted on staying, and no doubt he blamed himself.

"And he gets sad, sometimes, Rosa? He is kind to you, though? He doesn't hit you or anything?"

"Oh, Señorita, he is very kind to me, like a son." She lowered her voice. "But have you not heard the other problem—the curse of Pacal? Many people think he should leave the site. It seems to wear him down. I hear his cries in the night sometimes, the dreams."

"Oh, come on, you don't believe in that stupid curse? That's not why his wife died."

Rosa made the sign of the cross on her chest and kissed her thumb in response.

"When he has the bad times, I stay away. The drink, you know? Only once in a long while, maybe once, twice in a year. He isn't a *boracho*, a drunk, that's not what I mean. It doesn't last long, and I come back and we don't talk about it."

"You are a very good employee, Rosa."

"Oh, I am paid very well! My husband is gone and SinJin takes good care of my children and me. Do not feel sorry for Rosa!"

"Your English is unbelievable."

"Thank you very much." Rosa curtsied and smiled broadly. "The Professor has instructed me for many years. He says I am the best pupil he ever had."

"I don't want you to betray his personal life. I'm actually trying to figure out where the Professor works, if he has a storeroom here where he works on his artifacts, keeps his notebooks, that sort of thing. I would like to a chance to look at some of his finds."

"Oh, I don't know, miss. He might not like that."

"He would blame me. I wouldn't say a word, I promise."

Rosa thought for a moment and then leaned in, speaking softly. "I can't tell you where things are, but maybe if you found them yourself?" Tam nodded quickly. "There is a little hut behind the house. He locks it at night, but it might be open now."

Tam squeezed the woman's shoulders and painfully made her way to the back of the house.

A hut, very reminiscent of an ancient Mayan structure, hugged the palms at the far side of a powder-blue pool of water, a limestone sinkhole. Tam found the hut unlatched and ducked into the cool shade, her eyes slowly adjusting to the dim light. Pottery shards and tiny bits of jade and stone littered a table against the far wall. Tam took a quick mental inventory of each piece, noting the familiar mixture of Post-Classic materials and shapes. She pulled up a rusty chair and sat at the table, excited as usual at the prospect of examining Mayan finds. Gently, she touched each piece of jade and worked stone, and then turned to the pottery that was so special to her. Tam pulled her glasses from her pocket and put them on to distinguish between the old and new breaks in the pot, most worn with the centuries. She arranged the pieces into general groups, based on the writing coloring their surfaces.

Can't pull my weight, eh, handsome? You just watch me.

Tam wondered if Twaine knew he had a complete cup. It was small, but well made, with masterful brushstrokes in turquoise and coral-colored pigment covering every shard. She leafed through his dig notebooks, searching for any mention of the cup. The meticulous notes he made of each day's work, each find, each square meter of soil, mesmerized her. *He's top-notch, the best.* SinJin's careful observations enthralled her, and she understood within moments how he had earned his reputation as a preeminent time detective.

Hints surfaced, everywhere, that a royal family had lived in the area. Filled with excitement, she quickly sorted through the hundred or so shards. *Was there enough time?* She didn't have a choice, and certainly nothing to lose. Tam settled in to give Twaine the most beautiful restoration he'd seen, sure that once he saw his precious cup, he wouldn't consider sending her home.

"No, no, like this."

SinJin threw his hat to the ground in disgust and wiped the sweat from his brow with his once-white sleeve, demonstrating for what seemed like the thousandth time how he wanted the stones removed. This part of the Yucatan was sparsely populated, and with the exception of a few students from Mexican colleges who came only for a few days at a time, Twaine had only amateur workers. He thought bitterly of his colleagues in other parts of the Mundo Maya. They generally had a well-trained labor force with many men who had worked digs most of their lives. Their workers weren't formally educated, but were still some of the most talented archaeologists he had encountered. Most of the locals in this area had taken off for the Riviera Maya or Cancun years ago to make better money working at the resorts.

Damn, I'm so close. I need help. The rainy season threatened to start early this year, and all he had was a princess with bloody feet and a bad attitude. He laughed to himself, wondering how smug she was now that Rosa had informed her that her breakfast companion was her new boss. Well, *would have been* her new boss. He was still going to give her the boot.

"Señor! Andale! Hurry!" SinJin's heart pounded in his chest as he ran to the other side of the small ruined pyramid. Had they finally found an entrance to the tomb? He pushed his crew chief, Orlando, aside and brushed at the small opening between the huge foundation stones.

Orlando knelt close to SinJin and dug bare-handed with him at the rocky soil. "Is this it, boss?"

"I don't know." *God, I think it is!* "We'll have to clear away this vegetation and see if we can dig underneath these foundation stones. It won't be easy."

It wasn't. The crew of eight labored for hours, pulling away huge vines and boulders of limestone, trying to reach the bottom edge of the pyramid blocks.

Reluctantly, SinJin called a halt to work and started taking measurements in his notebook.

Orlando gestured excitedly. "We cannot stop now, Professor!"

"No, Orlando. This is when it's important to take it slowly. The wrong approach could damage whatever is inside. Only patience separates tomb raiders from archaeologists."

"I thought university degrees did that."

SinJin smiled wryly at his friend. The crew packed up for the day and left SinJin alone with his notebook, the flood of excitement, and the fear he didn't have the help to do the job properly. Plus, if he did have a King's tomb at Pacal, he needed to everything by the book, including the Mexican government's permission to excavate further. He needed Ramirez. SinJin packed his things quickly and dialed his friend's number as he began the drive home to Cozmano.

"Alberto Ramirez."

"It's me, Alberto."

"Ah, SinJin! You have some news for me, my friend?"

"Alberto, I'm nearly certain I've found a tomb. We cleared a tiny portion of the entrance of brush and vines and found glyphs that make it look very promising. It's all I can do to hold off until you get here." He laughed nervously, driving quickly down the treacherous road as he spoke on his cell phone. He tried to calm down, not wanting to betray such emotion to his Mexican colleague.

"I'll be down as soon as I can, SinJin. I'm a little tied up, but I'll try for tomorrow or the day after. Now you promise to pull back that damned enthusiasm and swear you won't touch the tomb until I'm there."

"Agreed."

"SinJin, the job offer stands."

"That's good, because I quit Princeton today. They wanted me back by next semester. I can't do it, Alberto. It's just not me; the stuffy classrooms, the kids they're putting through there these days, the endless meetings. You should see the bimbo they just sent me as an assistant."

"Yes, you need to be in the field more than anyone I've ever known. Then you'll take my university's offer?"

"Gladly. Thanks, Alberto."

"See you soon, my friend."

Ramirez hung up.

SinJin breathed in deeply, trying desperately to curb his excitement, to think clearly about how to prepare for the opening of the tomb. As he pulled into the drive of Cozmano, he remembered the blonde.

Taking the porch steps two at a time, he called for Rosa, sniffing in the incredible aroma of her traditional Mayan cooking.

"Rosa!" SinJin found her pulling fresh bread from the oven and hugged her tightly, laughing at her expression of surprise.

"What smells so wonderful?"

"Since we have company, so I thought I'd make your favorite, Pibil chicken. Did you have a good day on the site?"

"Awesome! *Asombroso!* Perhaps the best day of my life! I may have found what I'm looking for at Pacal—the tomb of Shield Jaguar. We'll see. Alberto will be here tomorrow or the next day, and he'll stay for a few days, at least."

"Professor Ramirez will come from Mexico City? Then this is terribly important!"

"He has to provide me with a permit to excavate further. I only had a partial nod from the government to do preliminary exploration of that section of the site. Understand?"

Rosa nodded enthusiastically.

"Rosa, where is the woman?"

"Tam. Dr. Tamara Martin. I have not seen her for hours. She went exploring, I think. Perhaps a swim in the cenote."

SinJin frowned. She couldn't have gotten far on those wounded feet. It wouldn't be very safe to swim in the sinkhole alone under any conditions, much less at night. He hurried to the back of the house and saw the light in the workroom.

"Son of a bitch!" His body tensed with fury as he strode to the hut and looked in.

She didn't hear him, but continued to work, glasses pushed down far on her nose, sweat dribbling in beads down her sundress. She sighed and stretched, then put down her tiny glue brush and gently rotated the wooden plank she had placed under the pot. SinJin watched in shock as she examined the exquisitely restored piece—a small cacao cup, one meant for a king. She read the turquoise and coral painted symbols aloud, almost reverently. "Spear Jaguar, son of Shield Jaguar." Then she pushed her chair back and sighed deeply.

Stunned, SinJin waited to hear if she'd say more. Could it really be the cup of Spear Jaguar—it meant he might be right about the tomb. If the son were at the site, would the father be far away? How had she put it together in one day? He had been putting off the job, sure it would be at least two days' worth of backbreaking work. How had she read the glyphs so easily? He would have needed to call in an expert. He rubbed his hand through his dusty hair as he watched her sketch busily in his notebook.

She stretched again, and this time, a different shock ran through him. He hadn't taken the time to really look at her this morning. Her legs went on forever, barely covered by her short dress. Her full breasts were falling out of her dress as she bent over the table, thinking herself alone. Her pale hair brushed her bare shoulders...*She's a bombshell, as beautiful as in the dream.*

"Damn it!" He pushed the metal door wide so it creaked loudly.

"Oh! You scared me! I didn't hear you."

"How dare you touch my notebooks? And my artifacts! Who the hell do you think you are?"

She sighed and rubbed her eyes. "All right. I took a chance, and it didn't work. I called you an asshole. Well, you are an asshole. A brilliant one," she indicated his notebooks with a sweep of her hand. "But an asshole, nevertheless. It doesn't matter how brilliant or hot you are. Nothing could make up for that horrible personality. I hope you *choke* on your King, Señor Suave."

"Which King?"

"Nothing else matters to you, does it? I know your type. Can't say I blame you, actually. Spear Jaguar, son of Shield Jaguar. Is that what you want to hear? You were hoping for the father, I see." She shoved the chair back under the workbench. "Lovely cup. Don't worry, I won't tell anyone. Congratulations—you've found your tomb. Will you give me a lift to the road tomorrow? My feet are still killing me."

SinJin saw her fight back tears—were they tears of anger or disappointment? Probably both. He didn't move from the doorway.

"How did you do that?"

"What?"

"Put that together so quickly? And read it. Are you sure of what it says?"

"Positive."

He pinched the bridge of his nose and squeezed his eyes shut.

"Tamara, is it?"

She nodded.

"You're fired."

"I know." She looked at the floor and hobbled toward the doorway, crying openly now. She didn't leave him any option but to move aside or be slammed with her body. He didn't move. She nearly bounced off him, but he grabbed her arms and steadied her. She took in a quick breath and looked into his eyes.

"I resigned from Princeton today." He laughed at her shocked expression. "You can't imagine someone doing that? They've instructed you to return immediately. Did you call me hot?"

"Resigned? But why now, when you might have found Shield Jaguar?"

"I might have found Shield Jaguar." SinJin let the thrill of the words sweep through him, then pulled himself together at the sight of Tamara's tears and confused expression. "Today seemed like a good day to let the Mexican Government know what I have down here. My friend, Ramirez, is in charge of all Mexican antiquities." He didn't elaborate, seeing she recognized the name. "I've accepted his offer of employment, as a Professor of the University of Mexico. He won't make me teach, thank God. Just some dog-and-pony shows, fundraisers and such. You said I was hot, I'm sure I heard it."

"Princeton's been pressuring you to come back and teach?"

He nodded.

"That's so short-sighted."

"Agreed."

"Won't Princeton make a claim on your finds?"

"They can't touch it. Not a dime of the funds came through them, and they don't hold the permit. They know the Mexican Government owns anything I pull out of the ground and they can't afford to piss off the Minister of Antiquities here, who happens to be my good friend. I don't want anymore politics. Ramirez is a straight-shooter, at least I think he is."

"I see. You can let go of me now, mate."

He moved his hands to her hips, wondering if she'd slap him, or respond.

"I don't think I want to let go of you."

"Listen, Professor, under any other circumstances, I'd be sweeping your precious finds off that table and giving you the time of your life. But I'm not much in the mood, after getting fired. So get your fucking hands off me now."

SinJin let go. She slipped by him and hobbled towards the hacienda.

"Shit."

She wouldn't consider it, would she? No, she was young, her entire career ahead of her.

He caught up to her in a few strides and grabbed her wrist.

"Dr. Martin."

"Fuck off."

SinJin put both hands on her shoulders and turned her to face him.

"Curb your foul language and listen to me."

Tam opened her mouth, as if to protest and he clamped a hand over her lips. They stood in near silence for a moment, and as if to fill the empty space, the cicadas sang out in rhythm with the gentle warm night breeze.

SinJin took in a deep breath and searched for the right words, the perfect words. "You have a choice. You can put that suit back on and take up your duties at some college, teaching the unappreciative urchins all about the wonders of the ancient world, probably never putting your full talents to use. Or, you can have a piece of Pacal, as a contributor. Not as a co-author, mind you. My assistant. Same pay as Princeton, *but* only one weekend day off. The work continues straight through the rainy season, inside the storerooms. You've only been here a day, so you don't know how isolated we are, how hard we work. It's no picnic, and Cozmano isn't the Plaza. I suspect I know your answer already, but I'll give you the night to think of a nice way to refuse my offer."

He tried to ignore the movement of her breasts beneath the thin fabric of her dress as she panted under his grasp. She was so close, the scent of her light perfume filling the air, heated by the warm night air. Her brilliant blue eyes grew huge, and she looked very confused. He slowly removed his hand and let it slide down her arm, taking a final opportunity to feel her smooth skin. It shocked him to realize he hadn't touched a woman since Laura, except to hug Rosa.

Doctor Martin, if you could read my mind, see my dream, how you'd be cursing me now.

Regarding him carefully, silently, she slowly pulled her arm away and stepped back. He saw her swallow nervously. It didn't seem in character, and he waited for the barrage of insults. They never came. Instead, she simply nodded.

"What does that mean?"

"I called you hot."

A sly smile crept to her eyes and he felt a tremor of hope and life stir in his gut, a sensation he never expected to feel again.

"I thought so. But I can't compete with Princeton."

"I came here for Pacal, for the tomb. Not for Princeton. I hate teaching the 'urchins', as you call them. And we'll see about that co-author clause, Professor."

"It's non-negotiable."

"Everything's negotiable, SinJin."

"Then you'll throw in that lap-dance, along with long hours sketching glyphs and restoring pottery?"

"Before the season's over, I'll throw in a lap dance." She turned her back on him and headed towards the house. Rosa stood on the veranda, motioning for the pair to come to dinner.

Before the week's over, if I have anything to say about it.

C C C

Except for comments to Rosa on her spectacular cooking, Tam and SinJin ate dinner in complete silence. Tam finished a wonderful pastry dessert and placed her napkin on the table. With a final sip of her coffee, she stood and turned, not intending to say a word to this strange, compelling man.

"I didn't expect a goodnight kiss, but a 'goodnight' might be in order. You *are* under my roof."

Tam scowled. "You're a horrible host. You offer me a job and then can't find a single freaking thing to say to me. No wonder you lose your assistants. You're not dangerous, you're pathetic."

"I can still withdraw that offer."

Don't fall for it, he needs you.

"Go ahead." She bit her lip to hide her fear and watched him carefully. He leaned back casually in his chair, running his hand through his thick over-long brown hair. Tam tried desperately to push aside the fact that SinJin Twaine was a perfect specimen. He'd managed to shower and put on a clean shirt, his damp hair gleamed in the candlelight, and that face... Suppressing a sigh, she reminded herself what an idiot he was. A complete, grade-A asshole.

"You're fired. I'll get Tyre up here. I've avoided that call long enough."

Tam's heart flopped in her chest, a chill ran through her veins. "Tyre Rasmussen? Figures you'd know the only archaeologist to get kicked out of Harvard for harassing his female students! Go to hell!" Tam braced herself on the table and leaned in closer to him. "Get Tyre Rasmussen, go ahead, ruin whatever reputation you have left. You tricked me on purpose, asshole! You let me believe you were some flunky for the great St. John Twaine and then pull this 'stay, I need you' bullshit. What's up with that? Well, Professor, your reputation precedes you, so I should have guessed. My friends all said 'find the biggest idiot in Mexico, and that will be the Ivy League Beast.'" She folded her arms in satisfaction.

"Ivy League Beast?" He laughed so hard he was barely able to speak. Rosa snickered as she cleared the table.

"Rosa, did you know what they call me back at Princeton?"

"Oh, SinJin, I've heard a lot worse names for you."

SinJin shook his head, still laughing. He was glorious when he laughed—his eyes sparkled and his entire face came to life, and Tam knew that she was probably better off a few thousand miles away from him. This guy might be zero on the personality scale, but he was a perfect ten otherwise, and she felt it, every bit of it. Tam wanted to crawl onto his lap, devour his gorgeous mouth, and run her hands on the smooth tan chest and stomach she'd seen the day before. Then slap that smug grin off his face. Yes, it was probably good she was leaving.

SinJin's laughter died down and so did his smile. He looked serious again and he concentrated on his wineglass, rubbing his finger around the rim. Tam watched his finger go around and around, started fantasizing about his touch as the glass began to sing. *He has the exquisite hands of an artist.*

"As I said earlier, you're a contributor, *not* a co-author."

Rosa giggled and SinJin scowled at the housekeeper. She wiped her hands on her apron and returned to cleaning up, but she didn't try to hide her grin.

Grabbing a bottle of wine, he walked to the far side of the porch and stretched out in a hammock, where he proceeded to drink straight from the bottle.

"And," he nearly yelled from across the broad porch, "If you call me an asshole one more time, you really are fired."

"Fuck you, Professor. Don't be surprised to wake and find me gone."

"If you're quite through, I think I'd like to drink myself into a mild haze. *Alone.*"

Chapter Three

Shield Jaguar chased her through the site of Pacal. Tam ran as fast as she could, lungs ready to burst, leg muscles straining, but he was gaining on her. Her tears burned her cheeks and she saw in horror that blood fell in drops onto her hands as she reached to wipe her tears. She opened her mouth to scream, but heard only his laughter as he grabbed her shoulders and spun her to face him. Struggling frantically in his grip, she finally managed to pull off his headdress and mask.

SinJin!

He was so handsome, she thought numbly, realizing he meant to kill her. He lifted the knife high and she pushed against his chest, but he pinned her against the rough stone of the pyramid wall. "I'm sorry, SinJin, please! I'll do anything you ask. I didn't mean to damage the burial!"

Too late. She felt the fire of the stone flint blade slice across her neck. She heard his dark laughter and screamed.

Tam started awake with a cry, to find Rosa shaking her.

"Oh my God. Rosa!"

"It's almost five! You really overslept, Tam. Hurry, he'll be furious. The Professor doesn't like to wait for anyone."

"What?" Tam took in a deep breath, remembering in shock that she was in Mexico, a hired hand of the Beast, and evidently late for work. Crawling out of bed, heart still pounding furiously and hands shaking, Tam gingerly tested her feet, a few steps at a time. Rosa stopped her and examined her soles. "Fresh bandages. Wait there."

She came back and treated Tam's cuts, handing her pills from her apron pocket.

"Trust me, Rosa, you *don't* want to see me on painkillers."

"Antibiotics. Take one in front of me, this very moment." Rosa shoved a glass of water in Tam's hand, clucking at her hesitation.

"Okay, okay, you're probably right!" After downing the pill, Tam pulled on clean shorts and a tank top, gathering her hair back into a ponytail. Rosa trailed her movements like a sheepdog.

"Rosa! I need a *private* moment. Okay?" She locked the door to the bathroom but could hear SinJin yelling from the porch.

"Where is she, damn it? Five minutes, Dr. Martin. After that, I leave without you!"

"What *is* his problem?" Tam cursed as she gingerly pulled on socks and hiking boots over her bandages. She grabbed a long-sleeved shirt and her gear bag, into which she shoved her camera, notebook and drawing pen, trowel, paintbrush, and sunscreen.

Rosa pushed a large canvas bag into her hand as she scurried onto the porch. Tam looked inside and saw a bottle of water, what looked like a ham sandwich, and a blessed thermos of coffee. She leaned down and kissed Rosa. "You're my hero, Mama."

Hesitating briefly on the porch at the sight of SinJin as he tapped the steering wheel impatiently, Tam uttered a quick prayer for strength. *He's not going to get to me, no matter what. You're a Martin, and Martins kick ass!* Tam took in a deep breath and jumped into the Land Rover. Without a greeting, SinJin roared down the road.

"Damn, forgot my hat!"

SinJin reached into the back of the Land Rover, pulled out an Aussie bush-style hat, and plunked it on her head. He looked at her in challenge, daring her to complain, but she vowed again not to give him the satisfaction.

"Thanks! You're the best boss in the *whole* world!" She smiled sweetly and noticed a brief snort of laughter from him. She was already having the time of her life, she thought in wonder. *I'm doing what I was born to do—right in the middle of the greatest Mayan discovery of the decade. The greatest Mayan researcher of the decade thinks I'm good. Well I am good, damn it.*

She whistled to herself as the scenery whizzed by in semi-darkness.

SinJin glanced at her. "Your feet?"

"Fine."

"Rosa gave you breakfast?"

"Yep."

"Hat fit all right?"

"It's perfect."

"It's three sizes too big. Looks ridiculous."

"I adore it."

"I don't personally give a damn, but you probably should wear long pants and looser clothing."

"Whatever you say, mate."

"I'm not Australian, I'm South African. We don't say mate."

"Okie dokie, mate."

"As I was saying, I don't care, but the crew is a bit rough around the edges. Not used to a beautiful..."

His voice dropped off and Tam bit back a triumphant retort. *Beautiful, he had said it!*

"You got it, chief."

The sun slowly ignited the sky, and the real glory of the landscape hit Tam. The site hugged a tributary of a lazy river, turquoise ocean water carving the middle of the deeper blue snake. Tam sighed in satisfaction, feeling more at home among ruins than anywhere else in the world. And these were *lovely* ruins, she noted with excitement, sitting up eagerly to get a better view of the site as they wound their way along a bumpy shaded road. Not the largest, not the most ornamental, but about as perfect a small Mayan world as one would ever see.

"This center served a few thousand occupants, maybe four?"

SinJin gave her a quick nod. "More like three. I don't yet know the full extent of the secular part of the city, but it likely doesn't extend beyond the river. I plan on getting to that, but for now..."

"First up, Shield Jaguar."

"If he's here."

He's here. And more.

Pacal was special, Tam felt it. She'd been on a dozen Mayan sites, some magnificent, some modest, all fascinating, but Pacal had a mystical feel. A shiver passed through her as she took in the ruins. Gnarled trees extended winding branches that looked like arms, reaching out from the rubble of tumbled pyramids and houses. Pieces of stone carvings littered the ground like petrified corpses. Vines partially hid likenesses of kings and gods. She nearly jumped when she noticed a huge snarling stone face peering from beneath dead leaves. Lizards emerged from their lairs to wait for the sun to heat up ancient foundations. Tam usually loved watching the slow moving creatures, but now they seemed to watch her. Shadows shrouded most of the site, and the air seemed thick. Sweat moistened her forehead despite the early hour, and she laughed at herself. *It's just a site, Tam. Don't let your imagination run away with you.*

"Pacal is like something out of one of Catherwood's drawings. Like no one has been here since the explorer himself."

"What a romantic. You belong with Tyre Rasmussen at Uxmal. He claims to have found some of Catherwood's drawings and his diary."

"Really! Oh my God, I have to get down there."

"Hmm. I'll tell him next time we talk."

"You sound a little worried. Afraid to lose your new assistant to your pal?"

"Dr. Martin, this verbal sparring is tiresome, and you aren't very good at it. Are you ready to hear about the site?"

"Yes, boss."

Tam turned in her seat to face SinJin, taking in his strong profile, scraggly hair, and thinking how ridiculous he would look in Shield Jaguar's headdress, how silly he would think her if she told him about her nightmare.

"The *Sacbe*, the wide way." SinJin indicated the direction of the great road that connected many Mayan cities. Then he gestured to the pyramid. "There's the largest structure, mostly unexcavated, but obviously Post-Classic, as is most of the site. There's a lot of reading for you to do on the far side of the pyramid. Over here are some buildings I don't yet understand, but I think they're probably religious. In that direction, around two hundred yards or so, is an area of fairly modest dwellings, probably secular. And there," he pointed to a shrub-covered hillock, "Is the source of the little jug you restored last night."

"Shield Jaguar's tomb."

"Well, let's not jump the gun. Ramirez will help us with that one. I can't break through until he's here—my permission to work the site depends on that promise. It's unlikely to be today." He sighed. Tam felt his tension, his burning need to know, his intensity. She hoped for his sake it would be the prize he sought. *No, hope for yourself, Tam. This is your break.*

They unloaded the Land Rover as the workers arrived, the sunrise now complete. Tam took in their workforce, mostly boys. SinJin glanced quickly at her, and she knew he waited for her to comment on their crew. She took extra care to greet each worker cordially in Spanish, and they seemed surprised when she helped them unpack their vehicles.

"Can I have a few minutes?" Tam asked SinJin.

"What do you mean?"

"To explore on my own. I want to take in the whole site, see the glyphs you talked about, check out the foundations over there. Only a few minutes, please? I know enough not to disturb anything, if that's why you're frowning."

"No, go ahead, it's fine."

Tam wandered in ecstasy. This would be her site, too. It was incredible—not as imposing as Palenque, or Uxmal, or the main centers, but rich in history, ready to spill its secrets. Tourists didn't care about the carvings as much as restored pyramids, but she saw that this site had important ones, and they were everywhere.

SinJin found her a full hour later, lying on her stomach to get a good look at a semi-hidden slab of stone.

"You're talking to yourself."

She ran her hands gently over the carvings. "I don't know why, it's easier when I read aloud. You know, 'See Spot run.' Didn't you ever read aloud, Professor?"

Tam suppressed a giggle, feeling his eyes drill into her back, and lower. Her shorts had ridden high on her buttocks as she squirmed along the steps, and Hot Stuff was taking a good look, she was sure of it

"Doctor." Yes, there was the annoyed snap in his voice.

"Hmm?"

"Get up. I need your help over here. We're clearing more of the tomb site and there are some glyphs that you could help me read."

"Hmm. One more minute." She continued muttering and squirming. "Take this down. One Smoke Rabbit, Two Smoke Monkey, Spear Jaguar..."

"I don't have a notebook on me. Get up!" He ordered more forcefully. "We'll come back to this, I promise." She backed out of the crawlspace and brushed herself off.

"Amazing stuff, simply amazing. Now, what were you saying?" She walked back towards the tomb and the workers, and as SinJin followed behind, she swayed her hips a bit and glanced over her shoulder, catching him looking. He glanced away quickly and coughed, pretending extreme interest in a bit of fallen sculpture.

They worked for hours, until the sun made it impossible to keep the laborers on their feet. They had removed most of the brush and some of the most recent outer wall of the tomb. Ramirez was nowhere in sight, so SinJin resigned himself to another day of wondering. Tam excused herself, intending to answer Nature's call behind a tree, out of sight of the men.

"Don't stray," SinJin snapped.

Tam looked at him curiously, wondering why he'd be worried about her moving out of his sight. She ignored him and walked to the far side of the ruined pyramid, the part closest to the jungle's edge. SinJin's concerned voice pulsed through her veins. 'Don't stray.' Was there something about Pacal he wasn't revealing? Tam felt an uneasiness sweep through her. *Ridiculous.* But she had to admit that she didn't want to be alone, not even a dozen yards away from the men. A breeze stirred the soil at the foot of the pyramid and Tam looked up, surprised. A clear, cloudless day. Where had the breeze come from? The branches overhead creaked and the leaves rustled. Then the noise stopped suddenly. Not even the caw of a bird. Tam gasped when she felt the hand on her shoulder and spun around. There wasn't a soul nearby.

"What the hell!"

She rubbed her arms to calm her sudden goosebumps. What was it Jack had said? Simply that the place gave him the creeps. Tam tried to shake off the adrenaline pumping through her system, but still felt wobbly and uneasy. It was the sun—too much, too soon, after her sunstroke and dehydration. She should be taking better care of herself. She made her way back to the Land Rover, not mentioning the encounter to SinJin, not willing to go back on the disabled list.

They climbed into the Land Rover and made the drive home in the blazing sun. Tam was surprised when SinJin pulled into a restaurant. She felt him looking at her, guessing he was daring her to argue with his decision.

"I want a cold beer." He announced his intention as if he dared her to question him.

"What a wonderful idea, Professor." Tam returned his look, wondering why he suddenly seemed angry again. SinJin strode ahead of Tam and took a seat at the edge of the outside cantina. He put on his glasses and opened a notebook, ignoring her completely. The waiter took their order and SinJin turned immediately to his notes, without a word to Tam.

So, this is how it's going to be. What the hell is his problem? Not bothering to hide her examination of him, she sat with her chin propped in her palm, leaning on the table. He was gorgeous, brilliant, very lucky, and terribly unhappy, with a bad habit of taking it out on people around him. She would get it out in the open, or they'd never get through the season together. She, for one, intended on getting through this season, and several more.

"Professor?"

He ignored her.

"Helloooo. Your assistant has a question."

He sighed, pulled off his glasses, and slapped his notebook closed. "Yes?" He looked at her with mock interest, eyes wide, hands clasped together in anticipation.

"Professor, what is your problem, exactly? And is there a drug for it?"

"That's your question?"

"Yes, that's my question." Tam imitated his pose and waited for the explosion.

"Right now, *you* seem to be my problem. I'm working. You are an interruption."

"You're unbelievable, SinJin, you know that? No wonder you drive everyone off the site. It's not going to work with me. You can fire me, but you aren't going to scare me off with those dark looks and rude words. Ooooh, the big scary Professor. Cut me a break." She snorted as she took a swig of beer.

He didn't say a word, but put his glasses on and opened his notebook again, teeth clenched tightly and eyes narrowed to slits.

Tam turned her chair so she almost faced away from him. She looked out to the beach and the turquoise waters lapping against the sand, wondering what would cut SinJin down a notch. What would make him drop the macho bullshit? What would make him more...mortal?

She turned back around and examined him openly again. This time he peered over his glasses and returned her stare. Damn, she thought, he even looks sexy in nerdy reading glasses. She let her stare wander to his chest, uncovered by his open work shirt, didn't bother hiding her appreciation of his body as she looked down at his flat stomach, and lower. Then she looked back at his face and leaned her head on one hand. He was starting to look uncomfortable, frowning and squirming a little in his chair.

Aha! It hadn't taken much—a little sexy visual tour, and the Beast was unnerved. Flirtation was certainly the key. What would it take to tame him? But she had to tread carefully. The man *could* actually fire her.

SinJin felt the heat flick at his body, praying she couldn't see how she had effected him, all day. Wearing shorts that barely qualified as shorts, showing off her incredible legs, wearing that thin top that hugged her like a second skin. What was her game? And actually staring at his dick! The girl had no shame. *The trouble is, you really dig that about her.*

"You're all dirty." He reached over and brushed some soil from the site off her cheek. Tam flinched in surprise at his touch. He looked away, wondering what had made him do that. He hadn't touched a woman like that in years.

"So are you. SinJin?"

"Hmm." He took a swig of beer.

"Am I going to be okay? I mean, do I have the skills you need?"

"You'll be all right."

"You'd want me for more than one season?"

Oh, God, it's been a day and she's talking about the season ending? She'll never stay. "We'll see."

They sat in silence for a few minutes.

"Professor, do you have a phone that works down here?" He nodded and flipped open his cell.

"I won't be long, and I'll pay you back."

"Doesn't matter." He concentrated on his notebook again.

Tam connected. "Jack, *guapo*! Yes, it's me. I'm fine! Yes, I'm staying. Princeton's already 'fired' me and I've been rehired. Honestly. Jack, the site is freaking unbelievable. I can't talk about the details," she eyed

SinJin as he straightened up at the mention of the site, "But you can read about me in *The Times*. Sweetie, can you call the parental units for me and tell them I'm okay, tell them I'll call them this weekend, that I'm staying on? Thanks, honey. Love you too." She flipped the phone closed. "Fast enough?"

"Who's Jack?" *I hate him. She has a boyfriend. Of course she does. What a fucking idiot you are, SinJin.*

"Jealous? You know him—Jack Peders. You evidently shot at him about a year ago."

"Oh, Peders. So you're great pals with Peders, thus the strong bias against me. The boy hates me, of course. I thought he was an intruder. He should have told me he takes midnight strolls. Terrible archaeologist."

"He's a man, not a boy, and he's *not* a terrible archaeologist. He may not be suited for the jungle, but he's great with the artifacts. He's a fabulous cook, too, but you already have one of those. Geez, what, you're like four years older than Jack? 'The boy.' How rude. What bias do I supposedly have against you? I'm here, aren't I?"

SinJin snorted and took another swig. "I'm at least six years older than your friend, but who's counting? So, you're spreading the word that you've lasted one day in my employ? Watch it—you'll get my reputation."

Tam laughed. "The Ivy League Beastess?"

"Very cute. So, you're tight with Peders?"

"About as tight as two people can be."

SinJin nodded and put his glasses back on. *Why so disappointed, SinJin? She wouldn't have a fling with you, she could have anyone on the planet. And she's your assistant. You'll get Rasmussen's reputation if you even consider it. But she did call you hot. I guess that doesn't mean shit to a flirt like her. Could have sworn Peders was...*

"You really didn't even *notice* Jack at all? Don't remember anything about him?"

"I'm not senile. Of course I remember him. Nice enough guy, nice looking I guess. Great resume. Seemed intelligent. I thought he was a little, well, gay actually..."

"There's no such thing as a little gay, Professor."

A breeze of unexpected, unwelcome relief washed through his whole body. Glancing briefly over his glasses at Tam, he winced at the amusement on her face.

"That's the first interest you've shown in my life."

"We were speaking of Jack Peders, as I recall."

"No we weren't." Tam smiled sweetly and took a healthy swig of her beer, then unexpectedly leaned in and brushed a bit of dust off SinJin's shirtsleeve. It took all his self-control not to grab her wrist.

"You talk a lot." He sighed and snapped his book shut. "All right, get it all out, everything you want to say, want to ask me. Let me guess, why am I such an asshole, an idiot, a beast—what else have you called me?"

"No, nothing like that. I was wondering if back at the site, when I was stretched out on the stairs, remember?"

He nodded.

"Well, did you like the sight of my ass as much as you seemed to?"

He did choke this time and shook his head in amazement, searching desperately for a good comeback, finding none.

"I thought so." She smiled smugly and brought the bottle to her lips, rubbing it along them slowly, then taking the top into her mouth suggestively.

SinJin felt himself blush for what might have been the first time in his life. He wanted to leave, but couldn't afford to stand and show the restaurant patrons what this girl had done to his body. He stared at the ground as if it were examining a precious artifact.

Tam snickered.

"Does that work on the boys at Princeton?"

"Every time."

"I've never met anyone like you."

"As my mother is fond of saying, the Martins kick ass. You ain't seen nothing yet, Professor."

"I can't tell if you're dying to stay or get fired."

"You're a smart guy. I'm sure you'll figure it out."

Chapter Four

After a silent ride home, Rosa greeted them with frozen margaritas and bowls of salsa, guacamole, and chips.

"I'm going to be a lush by the end of the season. I've never had a better margarita." Tam sipped the cool tart liquid and leaned back in the shade of the porch.

"Sinj?"

He nearly jumped at the nickname only his sister had ever used. "Hmm?"

"Have you ever, well, *felt* anything at the site?"

"Like what?" He had dreaded this inevitable conversation, knowing that Tam was sensitive enough, and a skilled enough archaeologist, to pick up the feel of Pacal.

"A breeze when there shouldn't be one. A hand on your back when no one is there. A dream."

"A dream of what?"

"A dream of a Mayan trying to kill you?"

He snorted and sipped his drink. "I think that's the margarita speaking. After your sunstroke, you're surprised you had a nightmare? It's a site, abandoned for hundreds of years. There's nothing there but stone and vines and a few lizards. And hopefully a few bones."

"Don't ever play poker, Professor. Why don't you want to talk about it? You've had the dreams?"

He hesitated, unsure whether he was ready to confide in her, in anyone. "Not recently. Well, not until last night. It's all suggestion. Stephens wrote about the mystical feel of Mayan sites decades ago, Catherwood romanticized them with his drawings, and we archaeologists, we're all romantics, I suppose. Drop it."

"I'll drop it, for now. How about the *cenote* out back? Is it safe? I'm dying for a swim."

"Yep, but it's deep. Not to mention the eels."

"Eew. Forget it."

"We're about thirty minutes from a good beach. Maybe tomorrow or this weekend."

She looked at him, pleading. "Oh, why not now?"

"I want to get some work done this afternoon. No way."

"You can work on the beach, can't you? Or I can take the Land Rover?"

"Hell no, you can't take the Land Rover."

"Oh, come on, Professor. Just an hour on the beach. Give me that much. I had a rough first day, remember?"

"Oh, all right, but we're not staying long." SinJin knew his grumpiness wasn't terribly convincing. Tam clapped her hands like a child and ran to change, giving him a moment to pull his thoughts together. When was the last time he had looked forward to a break from work?

Work was his solace, his passion, his only reason for being.

Tam emerged in minutes in a bikini top and shorts, and he didn't look at her, afraid if he looked, he wouldn't stop looking. She was as sharp as a tack, and he knew she was baiting him. He just wasn't sure why.

It was blistering hot when they arrived at Tortuga Beach. Yards of pure white sand stretched down to the shallow turquoise water. SinJin carried their cooler and blanket under a small cluster of trees that provided precious little shade. What was he doing on the beach at the hottest time of day, when he should be working? He hadn't bothered bringing his laptop from the Land Rover and wondered if it would melt in the sun. This was so unlike him, so irresponsible.

"Why is it deserted?"

"Perhaps because it's about a thousand degrees out? There aren't any resorts for at least a mile in either direction."

She stripped off her shorts and was in the water in a minute, splashing and laughing in delight as he sat on the blanket, watching her play like a child. Tam waved at him to come into the water and he shook his head. *Brilliant. You're going to die in this heat because you're afraid of your assistant.* He growled and peeled his shirt off, making his way to the water's edge, where he left his flip-flops, and dove into the pure bliss. He felt his sweat washed clean and began to relax, letting the gentle current carry him on his back.

When he finished his swim and worked his way up the beach to their blanket, he saw her. Face-down, topless. He could see a good portion of her ample breasts from the side and couldn't pull his gaze away, feeling an instant bolt of desire. Now what? *Fuck it, SinJin, grow up. You've seen breasts before.* He marched up to the blanket and laid a good two feet away from her. Thankfully, she didn't move. Maybe she was already asleep. He really hadn't had these issues with his other assistants, he thought. Of course, none of them had lasted more than a week, scared off by Pacal or him, or both. Tam Martin evidently didn't scare very easily.

"Sinj?"

Damn. "Yes?" He opened a bottle of water.

"Can you reach into the bag and get my sunscreen?"

"Here." He threw the bottle next to her.

"You can't manage to put some on my back?"

"Nope."

"All right then, grouch."

SinJin realized she was going to get up, was going to make sure he saw her naked.

"Oh hell, Tam, lay back down."

He squirted the slippery stuff on her back and vigorously rubbed a little on. *Coward, fucking coward.* He forced himself to slow down, pouring more onto his hands, covering her shoulders, her whole back, working his way down to her legs. It took all the control he had not to groan aloud when he reached her nearly bare ass.

"Satisfied?" He threw the bottle on the blanket.

"Not quite, Professor. You have amazing hands."

He groaned and flopped onto his belly, determined to ignore any more plays. A few moments passed, and he had control over his body again. She wouldn't let him have it for long.

"Don't you need any? You'll burn."

SinJin sighed. "For crissakes, Dr. Martin. Are you always this forward?"

"Whatever do you mean?"

"Never mind." The images tortured him. SinJin imagined her hands rubbing lotion on his back, on his legs, then moving to his chest, his stomach, lower. It was too much. He was only a man.

"Go ahead," he whispered weakly.

Then he died. Bit by bit, piece by piece, she tore him apart. Tam started at his shoulders and ran her slick hands down his arms, making sure she spread her arms wide that her breasts grazed his back. He took in a breath at the contact as Tam moaned aloud. She slowly moved down his back and ran her hands around his waist, then slid one hand under the band of his shorts until she reached the slight indentation at the base of his spine. She glided down his legs and finally worked on his feet, covering every point until he squirmed.

"Ok, turn over. You're already burnt on your back."

"No."

"Yes. You know you want to."

"I don't suppose you'll be shocked to see what you've done to me?"

He rolled onto his back, eyes squeezed shut, waiting for her to comment on his hard-on.

"I've never had a boss like you."

"Like what?"

"Like a fucking male centerfold. Any of your employees ever tell you how hot you are, Professor?"

"What a foul mouth."

She massaged the front of him even more slowly, and he finally had to let a groan escape as she rubbed his chest and stomach. She spent extra time on his nipples, pinching them playfully with a giggle, and worked her way under the waistband of his shorts until he felt her fingertips brush the fringe of hair. An inch in either direction, and he'd lose it.

"You're panting, Professor."

"You planned this, the whole thing. The trip to the beach, taking your top off, the whole sunscreen thing."

"Yep."

"You're *so* fired."

"I don't think so."

"God. Please don't stop, Tam."

"Hmm. Don't want to stop, Professor."

A warning bell sounded in his head from far away. *She's your assistant, and she's very, very good. She'll leave if this goes South, and it* will *go South.*

"Tam, I can't do this."

"What?"

"I can't do what you seem to want me to do." He looked into her eyes and then let his gaze wander to her breasts. Impossibly gorgeous breasts. Huge, and tanned like the rest of her, with hard rosy nipples begging for his mouth.

"I can't get involved this way. With my assistant, I mean. I just can't. You don't understand. What I'm really like. Oh God." He squeezed his eyes shut against the sight of her.

"The beast?"

"No, not that one."

"Professor Sin? What the hell? You're some kind of deviant?"

He didn't answer.

"You don't scare me. Okay, have it your way. There's always Plan B."

"I'm not sure I'll survive Plan A."

Chapter Five

SinJin finally dozed in the afternoon heat, woken occasionally by the movements of his companion as she returned from dips in the sea. When he finally sat up, he noted that she had pulled on a tank top and was grabbing some of Rosa's goodies from the cooler.

"Corona?" she offered.

"Sure, why not? Seems like we're going to drink all day instead of doing the work I needed to do."

"Grouch."

SinJin sipped silently, wondering when he *had* become such a grouch. He couldn't remember the last time he had taken an afternoon off and gone to the beach. Certainly not with a girl that looked like Tam. Not ever with a girl like her, in fact. He glanced at her. She seemed to have calmed down and returned to her role as his assistant.

"Do you think Professor Ramirez will come down tomorrow?"

"I sure as hell hope so. We really need him here. You're good with the glyphs, but he'll have a lot to say about them, and besides, it's his site, really. His country.

You'll like him." He snickered. "All the women do. He's got that Antonio Banderas thing going on."

"Oooh. I'm sure I'll swoon. Cut me a break."

"Tam, we have to talk."

"Hmm?" She munched on a piece of cheese.

He suddenly felt foolish, not sure how to broach the subject of her flirtation. He'd sound like an ass, asking her not to...not to what? Be sexy? What was he going to ask her to do differently?

"Never mind." He stood and started to pull their things together.

"No! I don't want to go home yet."

"You sound like a child." He was grumpy—hot, sweaty, hungry, thirsty, and horny.

"Come on Professor. I just got here, and yesterday was hell, and today was great. Let me play a little. I'll work my fingers to the bone the rest of the year. You know I will."

"All right, but we can't stay on this beach. It won't cool down for another hour, at least. You've had way too much sun in the last few days, and I can't afford for you to get sick. We have too much work ahead of us."

"How about town? I need to pick up a few things. You can stay in the shade."

"How could you possibly need a thing? That suitcase must hold enough for four women! Oh, all right, but I'm not going all the way to Playa del Carmen."

She put her hands on her hips in a parody of a stubborn child and stuck out her tongue.

"That's it, Doctor. The last favor I do for you. You've worn out your welcome. From here on out, it's archaeology, and nothing but. No shopping, no beach."

"No suntan lotion?"

"You're on probation." He couldn't hold back a laugh. How could a woman be so annoying and so much fun at the same time? Of course, it didn't hurt that she was beautiful, and smart, and a talented archaeologist, and had hands that could make a man get on his knees and beg.

Playa del Carmen bustled with tourists, even in the heat of the late afternoon. SinJin sat on a bench sipping a soda, feeling like a husband at a shopping mall while Tam ducked from one boutique to the next, dropping by every few minutes to dump a package on him before making her way into another shop.

"Ten minutes, then I'm leaving with or without you."

"After I bought you this?" She handed him a package and he stared at it blankly. A present? He slowly unwrapped it, laughing aloud. A tiny Mayan statue, a replica of the original he had excavated several years ago. It was a poor cheap likeness, but recognizable, nevertheless. A little monkey with a huge penis.

"Are you trying to tell me something, Doctor?"

"Oh, no, Professor, whatever could you mean?"

"Do you mean that I'm a monkey, or that I have a big cock, or both?"

He grinned at her and she grinned back. They locked gazes for a moment only, but the moment seemed to be frozen, and he felt a rush, a ripple through his chest. He wondered if she felt it too, because her eyes grew wide and misty looking.

"Oh." She mumbled something else and sat next to him on the bench.

"What?"

She wouldn't look at him, but took his soda and downed the last of it.

Well, congratulations, Tam. You got his interest. The problem is, he's got yours, big time. Idiot. With a stupid little gift, his eyes had softened to pools of needy brown, his sarcastic smirk was gone, and he seemed tickled pink. He dropped the statue into his shirt pocket and sighed.

"Thanks for the statue. You know that Rasmussen and I found the original at Uxmal?"

Tam arched a brow. "I read the excavation report. I'm a Mayan archaeologist, remember?"

"Of course you knew. That's why you bought it." He laughed lightly and sighed again. "I'm alone so much, I forget that the rest of the world reads what I write, sees my work, you know?"

Oh my God, he's lonely. The Beast is lonely. A stupid little gift had delighted him.

"Thank you."

"You said that already. It was only a hundred pesos."

"I guess it's the thought that counts."

She had only meant to tease him, lighten him up, put him in his place, maybe lure him into an affair to forget her own failed relationships, to satisfy her curiosity, her lust. But this? What was this longing, this joy in his company?

Don't do this, Tam, don't fall for him. He shut down, threw the key to his heart away, buried it at the site. He's your boss, and you need this job. You have to work by his side every day, live under his roof. Back off, you're playing with fire.

Tam grabbed her packages and threw them into the Land Rover. He hopped in after her.

"Where to now?" He seemed happy, even enthusiastic.

"I think I like you a little better when you're brooding. This is unnerving."

"What's unnerving? You're the one who wanted to play today! I don't get you." He sped down the main highway, whistling. The Beast was whistling! "How about dinner? I'm suddenly starving."

He continued whistling as he pulled into the long curved drive of one of the big resorts. Tam followed numbly as SinJin led her through the elegant lobby to the main open-air restaurant overlooking the turquoise sea. The staff all greeted him intimately. So, this was one of his haunts.

"Sinj? Let me change, please I'm covered in suntan lotion, and these shorts and shirt—this place. I didn't know we were going somewhere so upscale." He looked confused. "It's a girl thing."

He threw her the car keys and took a table. Tam went to the Land Rover and collected one of her new purchases, ducking in the lobby restroom to pull off her transformation. She returned fifteen minutes later in a colorful wrap-around dress, hair combed, lipstick on.

SinJin took her in slowly, head to toe.

"You look...nice." Looking away, he took a sip of wine and stared out at the sea.

"Nice? Please, I'll get a big head."

Tam sat patiently as the waiter poured a glass of wine for her, retreating quickly with a sharp look from SinJin.

He moved his chair close to her and stared into her eyes from beneath his dark brows. "Doctor Martin, you're playing with fire."

"That's interesting. I think I said the same thing to myself."

"You're beautiful, exquisite. I've noticed. Hell, how I've noticed. Has it occurred to you that we're living under the same roof, that we're going to be working side by side for months? If you keep offering, I'll eventually take you up on it. One of us would get hurt—it never fails. It would probably be you. Once it goes South, you'll leave, and that would be bad for the dig. But I'm only a man, and I can find another assistant when you leave."

"You're not serious. You wouldn't risk losing me and you'll never follow through on this ridiculous come-on of yours."

"No? You honestly believe I'm not up to a summer fling?" He squeezed his eyes shut and pinched the bridge of his nose. "Or even one night?"

"I don't think that's your style. You'd like to pretend it is, but I think the reason you aren't involved with anyone..."

"I don't give a damn what you think. You don't know me."

He took her hand in his and she tried to pull away, shocked by his unexpected movement. He grabbed it again, more surely, and brought it to his lips, brushing them delicately on the back of her hand, then on her palm, briefly running the tip of his warm tongue in a suggestive circle that set her nerve endings tingling. Tam inhaled quickly. He released her hand and looked into her eyes, challenging her to respond in some way. A slow smile crept to his lips, to his eyes.

SinJin held her gaze, never faltering. He kept staring as the waiter appeared and he ordered for them both. Tam's hands shook as she fumbled to close the menu.

"Stop it! Get that look off your face."

"I don't think so. You started it. What kind of professional are you, Dr. Martin? Don't finish a job once you start it?" His voice was dark and low.

"You shouldn't be doing this. I'm not...I wasn't..."

"Not serious? Wasn't it a few hours ago that I had my hand on your bare ass, rubbing it slick with lotion, moving up and down your inner thighs? I thought I saw you squirm a little. I'm quite positive it was you squeezing my nipples, stroking my chest, moving down my stomach towards my cock, which as I recall, was throbbing rather fiercely for you. Did I imagine that?"

Tam blushed furiously. He hadn't lowered his voice, and the couple next to them had heard every word he had said. SinJin snickered when the woman smiled broadly at

Tam and winked. Tam took a quick swig of wine and he refilled her glass.

"Well, Tam. Was that you on the beach? The girl with the huge breasts in my face, nipples pleading for my touch, back arched to show them off. Fairly proud of those tits, aren't you?" His voice was lower now, and she knew she was in deep trouble. She met his gaze, which still hadn't left her face. His eyes were dark, dark pools. He ran his tongue along his lower lip and Tam took in a breath, feeling as if his tongue had actually licked her. He had an evil smirk on his face as he whispered, "Read my mind." SinJin's face was pure, raw, desire. Smoldering, on fire. He was gorgeous, perfect, sexy. She was soaking wet and throbbing.

"What did you want on the beach, Tam, when you were rubbing me? Did you want to take my cock in your hand? Or in your mouth? Sure it would fit? No, not so sure, are you? Or did you want me to slide my hand down your stomach and rub your wet pussy?"

"Stop!" She jumped up. SinJin pulled her back down and then went about the business of eating his appetizer, as if nothing had happened. He laughed lightly through the meal, glancing in her direction to ensure she was still aware of him, flustered, hot.

"That was really cruel, Professor," she finally managed. The sun had begun to set and the sky was flaring gorgeous shades of pink and red. He had chosen a romantic spot. They had skipped the romance, she thought, and had gone right to the heart of the matter. She was shattered, barely able to sit still. Soaking wet, breathing heavily, exactly how he wanted her. Oh God, she hadn't expected this battering of her senses. The Professor, the loner, the genius, the centerfold. Which one was he?

"Professor, if you were my employee, you would be *so* fired."

"I don't think so." He did a great imitation of her. She smiled despite herself and met his gaze. He smiled back, and she felt a bit more relaxed. He'd simply been teasing her, getting back at her for the beach, for pushing him.

"Guess I had it coming. All right, we're even."

He reached over, ran his thumb along her bottom lip, and pushed it slightly into her mouth. "Not by a long shot. You rolled the dice, Dr. Martin. You are free to leave my employ at any time. But you changed the rules, and if you stay, you'll have to live by those rules now. The gloves are off. What were you thinking?" He snickered. "That I was a virgin? That just because I've devoted myself to work I don't remember how to fuck?"

She shook her head and looked at the table. "No, I didn't think that."

"One more thing."

"Geez. There's more?"

He laughed. "Yes." He pulled his chair even closer to hers and spoke softly into her ear. His breath was hot, sending chills through her. "I haven't been with a woman in two years, Tam. I know what you're thinking—poor SinJin. His wife died and he's been grieving for all this time, not able to touch another woman. Right?" She nodded, reluctantly acknowledging he was correct. "Don't get me wrong, it felt like that for a while. But Laura was leaving me, and we hadn't been together for over a year. It wasn't my baby." His voice was becoming darker with each sentence. "And do you know why she was leaving me?"

Tam shook her head, feeling as if she would cry any moment.

"She was leaving me because she hated Cozmano, hated Pacal, hated archaeology, and hated me. Do you know why she hated me? Because Pacal came first, and she came second. Pacal will always come first. That's why I'll never settle down with a woman. That's what makes me a beast."

"No it doesn't." She was barely audible. "If Pacal were mine, nothing would be more important." He pushed back in his chair, looking incredibly confused.

"You don't mean that. No woman could feel such passion for my site."

"It's my site too now. I felt passion for it the moment I saw it." *And for you, St. John Twaine.*

He took in a deep breath and looked at her closely. "Well, Pacal is partly yours, I suppose. Just a very, very tiny part of it, understand?"

She smiled weakly. "I know. Why else would I put up with you?"

"Ah. That's right, I'm your meal ticket to fame and fortune."

His eyes betrayed his disappointment.

"No." She reached up to his face and rubbed her hand along his jaw. "I want my piece of Pacal, that's true."

81

SinJin turned away.

"Listen to me, Professor. How could I not want to be a part of Pacal?"

"Of course." He nodded quickly, waving her off to change the subject.

"No, SinJin. I'm not finished. There's something else I want. How could I not want a piece of *you*? A woman would have to be dead not to want you. But you are the weirdest guy I've ever met and you actually do scare me a little. You have pretty high standards. I don't know if I can satisfy you."

"Satisfy me? Are we talking about work or sex?"

"Well, there's the impossibly demanding excavation director."

"And?" He arched a brow in question.

"My lover."

"Isn't that a little presumptuous. All we've managed is a bit of childish flirtation."

"Maybe premature, Professor. Presumptuous, no, I don't think so."

SinJin sat back and groaned. "How did you turn this around again? You're very talented, Doctor Martin."

"That remains to be seen."

Tam toasted her glass against his, wondering if she had lost her mind. Falling for the Ivy League Beast. And probably headed towards looking for a new job when it went South, which he promised it would.

Chapter Six

SinJin glanced at Tam, who was fretting over a fingernail as she looked out the window of the Land Rover. The stunt on the beach had been all bluster. She didn't know what she wanted. Should he let it go for now? His body ached and his cock still throbbed. And he needed something more from her. He couldn't put his finger on it. SinJin shook off the feeling—ridiculous. What could he need from her besides a good lay? God, he felt like a damned teenager. Maybe he should ask her to go steady first, he laughed to himself. *Stall, SinJin. If you make a real move, if she falls into bed with you, you might lose her. Pacal needs her more than your cock does. Think about this.*

"One last drink," he asked as they made their way up to the porch.

"How many does this make today?" Tam laughed. "I've lost count."

"I don't think I've actually finished any of them." He grabbed two glasses and a bottle of wine from the living room and brought them to the porch bench. They sat in silence, listening to the jungle noises. SinJin was surprised how comfortable it felt to have her next to him, how comfortable he was sharing his refuge with a woman again.

"Quite a spot you have here, Professor. And all to yourself."

"Yes, I'm usually alone here this time of day. This is my ritual, sitting here, mulling over the dig while I listen to the night noises of the jungle. Sometimes I think I hear the growl of a wild animal, fancy it's a jaguar. But as I said, we archaeologists are all romantics." He sighed, wondering why his evenings alone now seemed rather pathetic as he spoke about them. "It is quite a spot."

"I'm jealous. How old is this house? When did you buy it?"

"It was my father's. This was a small plantation over a century ago. The area west here was all cultivated, but it's grown back. My parents came here often, back when there wasn't a resort within fifty miles."

"He wasn't an archaeologist, though?"

"Oh, hell no. Thought archaeology was for hacks. For people who couldn't make it in business."

"And did you ever try? To make it in business? His business?"

SinJin stole a sideways glance at her. "Why are you interested? Why am I telling you?"

"You're interesting. Or hadn't you figured that out? You've been down here too long, Professor. You need a little perspective. You're the stuff of legends back home. You do realize that?"

"I go back once in a while. I'm not that eccentric, Tam, not a complete recluse. People like Mayan archaeology.

They spend a week at a Cancun resort, spend a day at Chichen Itza, and think they understand. They love to listen to me talk about antiquity. But I hate those lectures. They crave stories of mystery and majesty, have no real interest in the nuts and bolts of the field."

"Oh, come on. You can't hate it that much. You're the best at sharing your research, of making it understandable to the public."

"Perhaps I hate that they attach the mystery to me. It's silly."

"Oh, I see. Lots of women after Indiana Jones, eh? No one loves poor SinJin for himself. If he were pumping gas, no one would even notice him."

"Drop the psychoanalysis, Tam, it's not your strong suit."

"Oops, a little close for comfort. Listen, Professor, you know you're exquisite, brilliant, and successful. Why are you alone here? What's the problem?"

"Who says there's a problem?" What *is* the problem, he thought, lifting his glass to his lips.

"So, Dad was a businessman. And Mom?" Tam wasn't giving up.

"She was a saint. She could have done so much better than him. And maybe she would have, but I came along."

"And did she like Cozmano?"

"Loved it. She wanted to live here permanently. She was the one who really adored Mexico, and ancient cultures. When other kids were going to the park, she was dragging me to museums and archaeological sites.

Greece, Italy, Egypt." He sighed. "I suppose I'm living her dream."

"You miss her terribly."

He didn't comment, didn't need to.

"Well, she had good taste. I can't imagine why anyone would ever want to leave this place. It has a feel of...I don't know the word for it?"

"Rightness."

"*Rightness.* That's it exactly. The house, the jungle, the sounds, the smells, the region. It's perfect. I really am jealous."

As a matter of fact, he thought, it's more than right with her here. It's *perfect.* He finally knew what he wanted from her, and it stunned him. He wanted her to stay, to sit with him on this porch, to be by his side at the site, to lay with him, to be his friend.

"I suppose I have become a beast. Why don't you seem to mind?"

Then he did the unthinkable. He held her hand. SinJin closed his eyes, terrified she would pull away, laugh at him. She did neither. SinJin felt electricity run through his hand, all his nerve endings lit up. He saw Tam look at him in surprise and closed his eyes.

"Professor, do you know how complicated you are? And how wonderful? You are simply wonderful."

"Tam." He turned, looked into her lovely blue eyes, and felt the world fall away, as if they were the only two souls on the planet. He moved to kiss her, but she didn't give him a chance. She rose and left him alone on the bench.

Shit. So she did scare, but not with threats and insults. No, he'd scared her by holding her hand. He finished his drink and ran his hand through his hair, suddenly tired. At least he knew where he stood, and they'd go on tomorrow as if nothing happened, as if nothing mattered but Pacal and archaeology. *It's best this way, SinJin. Get over it.*

He entered the house, pulling the door closed behind him. Then he saw that her bedroom door was open, revealing the flickering of a candle against the wall. He looked in. She sat on the bed, still fully dressed. She met his eyes and smiled nervously.

"Close the door, Professor." He pulled it shut and sat next to her.

"What's going on, Tam? You're confusing the hell out of me."

"I *am* just a little afraid of you. You're a hard guy to understand."

"Then why invite me in? Dr. Martin, do you really want me here?"

"Yes, I want you here. Very badly, in fact."

"To keep your job? I don't work that way."

"Nor do I. Give me some credit."

"Then?"

She tentatively ran one finger down his cheek, to his neck, and down his chest. He caught her hand quickly.

"Tam, I'm not sure this is a good idea."

"Do you care?"

Oh, God, yes I care. I don't want to ruin whatever chance I have to make you stay with me.

He pushed her back onto the bed and bent over her, brushing his hand through her silky pale hair. When he moved closer to her, let his body meet hers, the thrill made it hard to think. *Come on, SinJin, keep your wits about you.*

"I have to care. I'm responsible for the site, and in a way, for you. You're my assistant, but you're not my assistant for life. You have your whole career ahead of you. I don't want to interfere with that, or with this season." *You fucking liar, SinJin.*

Tam's eyes grew misty, and he wondered if she were about to cry, but she smiled wanly and nodded. "One night. I don't want more than that. In the morning, we're director and assistant. No strings, no questions. We'll just get it out of our system. Hey, it might not even be that good! Then it's back to kicking ass at the site. I'm not a student anymore, and you're not my professor, SinJin. You can't get in trouble. It's a win-win, right? One night."

"I see." SinJin felt a wave of unfamiliar panic rush to his brain. 'One night. I don't want more than that.' *But I do, damn it.* Could he be so fucking amazing in bed that she'd change her mind? He hadn't been enough for Laura. His heart sank. *Laura.* She'd taken a lover—what did that say about him? What hope did he have with this goddess looking up at him, this bombshell?

"What chance do I have of ruining you for any other man?"

"Such an ego." She laughed, but he caught her laugh with a kiss and it turned to a moan. Heaven. She was heaven. The taste of dark wine; the smell of sun, skin, and soap. Tam grabbed his hair and deepened the kiss. She took control, and he let her, stunned at how he enjoyed letting go, letting her guide the kiss. The way she used her tongue, her teeth, her lips, to steal his breath away—he'd never encountered eroticism like hers. He returned her passion and doubled it, exploring her lips and tongue, groaning as the kiss hardened his cock, as she moaned in response. They both panted and lavished one another with quick pecks and nibbles.

SinJin moved to her neck and bit and licked until she struggled against him, reached down to caress his swollen cock. "Oh, please, let's do it." Her hot whisper into his ear pounded to his cock and he felt his control slipping quickly.

He pulled away, and Tam looked puzzled. SinJin pulled off his shirt, knowing that she loved the look of him. Thrilled that she loved the look of him. It was an incredible turn on, and he had never allowed himself the luxury of this kind of adoration before. *Please God, let this be right.*

"Two years, Tam. Think about it. Do you want to be the first in two years?" He pulled off his shorts and briefs in a swift movement. He saw the effect he had on her, the appreciation, the lust.

"Pleased? Or disappointed?" He looked at her darkly from beneath the hair that had fallen into his eyes.

She groaned and reached for his thick swollen cock, jutting straight to his navel. He moved back a step as she reached for him.

"No wonder you're vain, Professor. I want that, now." Tam stood and untied her halter dress, let the silk slip to the floor, leaving her in a tiny patch of black silk.

"Oh, God help me." SinJin's knees nearly buckled at the sight of her. "You look like a stripper. Actually, you look better than any woman I've ever seen. Jesus, Tam."

"Get over here, Professor."

She reached to touch him and he backed up again.

"Keep talking to me, Tam. Say anything at all. How do you think I've gotten by all this time? Alone, at night, in my bed, thinking of what I want to do to a woman, what I need her to do to me." He rubbed his chest and slowly brought his hand down to his cock, teasing himself in light strokes and breathing in quickly at his own touch. He squeezed his eyes shut and tilted his head up, moaning slightly, shocking himself a bit at his exhibitionism. *My God, I've never touched myself in front of a woman. Why does it feel so good?*

"I wonder," he hissed, "What it looks like when you do this to yourself. What do you do to yourself, Dr. Martin? Have you touched yourself under my roof? Do you rub yourself slowly or quickly? Do you take your time, or do you make yourself come hard and fast? Maybe you get a little help? Do you like toys, Dr. Martin? No? Never had a toy? We'll have to fix that."

Her eyes betrayed her.

"Oh yes, you will, for me. You'll do anything for me." He approached the bed and pulled her up, licking her mouth and neck, biting her ear and flicking his tongue inside briefly to hear her intake of breath. He pinched at her hard nipples and then leaned down to suckle on one as he cupped the other breast. She clung onto him tightly, crying out in desperate need. Running his hand down her smooth belly, he cupped her pussy, feeling the heat and dampness of her lust.

Tam ran her palm down his stomach, capturing his cock in her palm. He bit back a cry. "Kiss me again, Doctor." She pulled at his tongue with her lips as she ran her hand around the smooth tip of his cock. Sheer bliss, sheer instinct made him push her down to her knees. He heard her snicker as if from very far away and he looked down to see her staring up at him.

"Oh my God, suck me off, honey. Oh my God."

"Don't rush me, boss."

She used her hand first, sliding it around the tip and circling the shaft, then rubbing up and down. He shuddered in pleasure. She brought her hot tongue onto the tip, licking in circles and rubbing her lips back and forth until the sensation was more than he could bear. He pulled her head in and she finally took as much of him in as she could, sucking and sliding her tongue around him, rubbing the head on the back of her throat.

"Oh, Tam, my God. Stop now."

"I don't want to stop. I don't want to ever stop."

SinJin pushed her away and then led her to the bed, legs shaking, heart pounding. Every ounce of his being screamed to take her, to fuck the living daylights out of her, and never stop. But he had to wait, he had to leave her wanting him.

SinJin rolled onto his back and she fell onto him again, sucking him in as she stroked his shaft.

"Doctor, I'm going to come in a second if you keep that up."

"That's the idea."

"I want you to know something."

"Tell me. Tell me anything."

He gasped the words out. "I'm ashamed to say that I'm a hopeless tease. It's a sickness. I suppose I deserve every nickname I've been called." He shut his eyes and groaned loudly as his world spun out of control, his orgasm pounding through his body in huge waves of release. He shuddered and pulled Tam into his arms, kissing her head, rocking her back and forth, as he reeled in ecstasy. After minutes of holding her, he gently extracted himself from her embrace and grabbed his shirt. He wiped his cock and stomach, and gently wiped Tam's chin and hands. He leaned and kissed her on the forehead.

"Good night, Doctor. Thank you very much for that. I'll have to consider giving you a sign-on bonus."

"You're not serious. You're going to leave me like this?"

"Like what?" He snickered mischievously.

"Throbbing, aching, soaking wet, crazy for that body and face of yours."

SinJin pulled on his shorts and kneeled at her bedside. "Dr. Martin, as you no doubt observed, I don't like to hand out compliments readily. But you are the sexiest woman I have ever known. And I think you feel the same way about me? Now, I wonder," he whispered, as if conspiring with her. "What do you think it would be like if I actually touched you? If we actually made love? Hmm?" Taking in a deep breath and one last look into her eyes, he turned and left the room.

SinJin flopped onto his bed and sighed. It had taken every ounce of control he could muster not to luxuriate in her unbelievable body. But he *had* to have more time, more of her. He hoped it was enough, that she would want another night with him. That she would lay awake and wonder what it would be like. That she would stay. *She has to stay. I hate how much I want her to stay.*

☾ ☾ ☾

"And did she stay, Lord? Please tell me she stayed!"

Shield Jaguar laughed and rubbed his hand along A'ok's smooth back, pulling her in closely.

"So impatient! You will have to wait to find out. Do you want to hear more?"

"You are cruel! What must I do to hear what happens?"

Shield Jaguar poked his tongue into his cheek in an imitation of A'ok. She sat up and crossed her arms petulantly. "Well? What?"

"I think it is time for you to put that mouth to use at something other than endless babble. And afterwards, I'd like my pipe and my cacao cup. Very sweet."

"You are insufferable, Lord." But a sly grin crept to her lips as she licked her way down his torso and pressed the head of his cock into her mouth. He moaned in exquisite

pleasure, not caring what the priests thought of the sounds emanating from their quarters.

A'ok pulled away and slapped him lightly on his stomach. "For the love of Chac, do not stop your story!"

Shield Jaguar laughed loudly, caressing her hair, wondering at the love that welled up in his chest. "I'm to speak while you bring me to fulfillment?"

"You are quite talented, Lord, I'm sure you can manage it."

He pushed her head back down onto his member and continued his story, breathlessly.

Chapter Seven

Tam wasn't ready to face the morning. Four-thirty, dressed and ready for work. How could she saunter onto the porch and have breakfast with him? Was she supposed to pretend last night hadn't happened, simply talk about the weather or their work? She couldn't have gotten more than two hours of sleep, spending most of the night staring at the ceiling, lusting after SinJin. The son of a bitch.

SinJin didn't look up as she sat at the table. He continued to scribble in his notebook, head leaning on one hand. She found his glasses even more attractive today, knowing how erotically he had behaved only hours earlier.

"How's the nutty professor this morning? I suppose you slept quite soundly." SinJin glanced over his glasses at her as if he had no idea what she was talking about.

Rosa emerged onto the porch and set a wonderful breakfast of eggs and sausages and fruit before her. Tam turned to the food, pushing it around on her plate, trying not to glance at SinJin every few seconds. It was so quiet, she could hear the tick of her watch. She was ready to rail at him, when he pulled off his glasses and looked up.

"What's the sequence of the glyphs you read yesterday?"

"Huh?"

"The glyphs. You know, those funny rounded symbols the ancient guys carved on the buildings. It was Smoke Rabbit, then who?"

"Oh. One Smoke Rabbit, Two Smoke Monkey, Spear Jaguar, and I think the next was Shield Jaguar, but I couldn't see well enough to be sure. I guess that would be the reverse order of their rule. Hmm. That's odd."

"Exactly. I want you to spend more time on those today. Ramirez is coming tomorrow; he left a message on my cell. A big mess over a site in Belize that the University is excavating. God, it had better be tomorrow. I hope he's not putting me off for some reason. It's not like him to take this long." He went back to writing for a moment, then abruptly shut his notebook, drained his coffee cup and began pulling his backpack together.

"Ten minutes." He went inside.

So that's how it's going to be, Tam thought, fuming. We'll see about that. "Asshole," she said loudly, knowing he would hear her.

They rode to the site in silence, and despite her annoyance at SinJin, Tam felt the same excitement when she saw Pacal for the second time. She couldn't wait to get back to the glyphs, to read the story that the ancient inhabitants of Pacal had written on the stairs of their temple, the story that hadn't been read in hundreds of years.

As they began unpacking their gear, terrified cries from the workers echoed across the site. SinJin grabbed Tam's hand and they ran to the far side of the pyramid. Tam could barely take in the horror.

Blood! Deep red blood. Everywhere, not even dried in places—it had run in tiny streams from the top of the building to the bottom stair and onto the soil. Tam felt nausea rise up at the smell and the ghastly sight of it. Someone must have used gallons of blood. Flies swarmed on small wet patches. On one large stone, she saw the symbol for the gods of Death, the guardians of Xibalba, drawn in the deep red. The workers chattered hysterically. Some threw down their shovels, swearing to leave the site for good.

SinJin cursed and while he turned to the crew, interviewing them about the vandalism, Tam sat on the ground and took in the horror. Who would do such a thing? A warning, obviously, but from whom? The site was so desolate, it couldn't be children. One of the workmen?

SinJin had managed to calm the men down, all except for one, Rosa's nephew, José. He wouldn't pick up his shovel.

"No, *Señor*. Cozmano, you, Pacal. All very bad. The King will not let us wake him. He speaks to me in the wind. Leave him be." He walked to his bike and took off down the path towards the main road.

SinJin ran his hand through his hair and cursed up a blue streak.

"Who did this, SinJin? Why?"

"How the fuck should I know?" He kicked the dirt.

"I know. It's a sacrilege. And a warning?"

"Absolutely. A childish one. Did you hear that?" He turned to the workmen. "Only a child would do something like this. No true Mexican would do this to his own heritage! If you know who did this, tell him that he is a fool, and it won't work. I'm not leaving. Pick up your shovels and start where we finished yesterday, or you won't get paid today." He stormed off into the jungle. Tam longed to follow him, to comfort him, but she recognized the fury burning through him. If it were she, Tam thought, she would want time alone to burn off steam. She'd let him handle this his way.

"Miss?"

"Yes?" She turned to Orlando, the head of the crew, who looked close to tears.

"It is not one of us, do you understand? We love the site, and the Professor, he is good to us. Better pay and hours than any other site, much better. We are not the best crew, you think. Too inexperienced. But we are getting better, you see? You must trust us. We could not hurt Pacal. Understand?"

"Sí, Orlando, I understand. Thank you. Please don't worry, I will tell the Professor." Tam believed the earnest man, and something told her this wasn't an innocent prank. She went back to the Land Rover to fetch her gear.

"Leave, now!"

Tam spun around, shaken by the voice that hadn't sounded real, hadn't sounded human. It had come to her on a light breeze, a whisper with no source. Her heart sank and tears welled to the surface. The curse. The hand on her shoulder, the blood, the voice. Impossible. There was a rational explanation for everything.

"Who are you? Come out, you chicken! We're not leaving."

Tam watched SinJin at the edge of the jungle, speaking in rapid-fire Spanish on his cell phone. Tam wondered what to say to him. Should she tell him about the voice? What would he think? No, the blood was enough for one day, and he was still furious, not ready for any tales of a curse.

Pulling herself together, she wiped her tears and went back to the bloodied ruin. Resolving to appear strong, she studied the vandalism. The color had made it easier to read some of the glyphs, highlighting the raised surfaces. She took out her notebook and started sketching, intending to make the best of a horrible situation. She felt SinJin by her side, but she continued working.

"Tempted to leave?" He sounded bitter.

"Why do you say that?"

He pointed to the blood.

"Oh. I thought you meant something else." He looked at her in concern, and she shrugged and continued her sketches.

"What, Tam? Tell me. If there's something else, I need to know."

"There's nothing!" she snapped. "Oh, SinJin, I'm sorry. It's just upsetting. Did you talk to Ramirez?"

"No, damn it. His secretary said he's still in Belize. I can't open the tomb, and now I've got this mess on my hands."

"Well, the workmen, except for Rosa's José, are all okay, I think. Orlando wanted to make sure we trust them."

He nodded. "I'll talk to them some more, and I think I'll let them go home today. There's not much they can do without Ramirez here anyway. I'll pay a few to guard the place tonight."

"Is that safe for them?"

"Sure, if they're armed." He patted his hip and she realized that he carried a gun under the long-sleeved shirt that she had thought only shielded him from the sun. "Game for staying a while?"

"Of course." She pointed to the glyphs. "I can read them better now."

He snorted. "Well, it's not a complete loss, then. Tam, thanks. You Martins *do* kick ass."

Two hours later, Tam sat in the dust, unable to sketch a moment longer while standing. She was soaked with sweat and covered with grime, but exhilarated. The glyphs had made her absolutely sure that they were at the location of Shield Jaguar's tomb. She was thinking of the best way to tell SinJin, imagining his face, how happy he would be. How proud he would be of her. She would share his most important moment. She closed her eyes. He would hug her, perhaps kiss her. Remember this day for the rest of his life.

"Leave!"

The hissed warning jolted Tam out of her fantasy. Her blood turned to ice water. She wanted to scream, but couldn't form a sound. Her legs felt as if they would give out as she scrambled to her feet. A warm breeze stirred and the soil spiraled up around her legs, threatening to surround her in a cloud. She ran in terror.

"SinJin!"

He caught her with one strong arm as she rounded the corner of the pyramid. "What happened?"

"A voice, warning me to leave Pacal."

"Whose voice? Where?"

"I don't know. It didn't sound, well I can't explain it." She turned away from him, embarrassed that she would sound ridiculous.

"It didn't sound human."

She gasped and looked him in the eyes. "You've heard it! What's going on? Tell me now!"

"If I knew, I'd tell you. I've only heard it twice, both times very recently. I don't know what it is, but I don't give a damn. Nothing has hurt me or anyone on my crew in four years."

"It's the tomb. Because you're closer to opening the tomb! Admit it! You think the same thing."

"The curse is bullshit, and you know it. Come on, it's someone playing a very nasty trick on us. Some people think Americans shouldn't be digging on Mexican soil, you know that. They resent our funding, our training. Don't think that we're loved everywhere we go."

Tam nodded uncertainly, remembering a similar vandalism incident in Guatemala. Maybe he was right, but she wasn't convinced.

"Come on, that's it for today. I've got to go over about four days of notes and you have some drawings there we can go over, right?" She nodded. They packed up and left Pacal to its guards.

"Why do you carry the gun if there's no threat here?"

"There's enough evil in the world without ghosts, Tam. Or hadn't you noticed? We're sitting on finds that have a fairly good black market value."

"Have you ever had to use that gun?"

"Only on Peders, your friend." He laughed. "And a few others." She looked at him quickly and he smiled. She wasn't quite sure he was kidding.

Tam relaxed a bit after lunch and a beer at SinJin's favorite roadside cantina. She suspected now that this was his ritual—a hot day at the site and an afternoon beer to quickly write some notes. She loved it, and tried to imagine spending all her days just like this one. The pleasure of that fantasy shocked her. Did she really want that? To spend every day working with him? For how long?

The memories of the previous night poured back in a flood and she couldn't think of anything but the site of him, pleasuring himself, rubbing his hand up and down his cock, face turned towards the ceiling in ecstasy. And there he was, right next to her, writing in a notebook as he had done at breakfast, glasses pushed down on his nose, taking occasional breaks to take a swig of beer or dig into the plate of nachos. Was this the same guy? Oh yes, it certainly was, she thought, seeing his smooth tan chest through his open shirt, his large arm muscles barely hidden by the worn fabric. He peered briefly at her over his glasses and smirked. Well, at least he couldn't read minds. She wondered what her next move should be.

"Tamara?" He took off his glasses. "Tell me about the glyphs you studied today."

"Oh my God, I almost forgot, because of the vandalism! Well, never mind that." SinJin listened to her analysis and grew visibly more excited with each word as they meticulously examined her drawings.

"Dear God, it really is him. You agree?"

"Congratulations, Professor. You've done it."

Tam watched in glee as a wonderful, excited smile crossed his face. He ran his hand through his hair in a gesture she was starting to adore and sat back with a big sigh.

"I always thought...but I worried that I might be wrong, you know? After four years alone, four years without a real colleague, you wonder about that line between your own hopes and dreams and reality. Rasmussen was skeptical when he visited, thought the site might be a bit too modest, and at times I agreed. Thought I might be kidding myself, seeing clues that weren't real. Until you came."

"Me?"

"When I saw you in the work shed, saw your restoration of the cacao cup, heard you reading the glyphs, I felt more than..."

"What?"

"Hope, I guess. For the first time in a long time, I felt optimistic. Like things might work out finally."

SinJin closed his eyes for a second, pinching the bridge of his nose. Tam longed to kiss him, beg him to let her in more, to keep talking. He hid so much longing, so much desire. What did he really hope for? *No, don't ask. Don't even think in those terms.* But she couldn't help herself.

"Do you ever hope for more?"

"More? More than the tomb of Shield Jaguar? What the hell else could I need?" She'd hit a nerve, she was sure of it. His voice took on the sharp edge she'd heard often enough in the last few days.

Quickly downing a long swig of beer, he turned back to her notebook, running his hand across the page that held the drawing of the King's name.

"I'm sorry to hear that, Professor."

"That I'm satisfied with my career? With where and how I live? I've dreamed of the day when I'd be sure, dead sure it was Shield Jaguar. It doesn't get any better than this."

"Sure it does."

They locked eyes for a moment and Tam's heart turned in her chest. *I could kill you, SinJin Twaine, I really could. You should be kissing me right now, telling me how much you like me, how much you want me to stay.*

"Stifle, Doctor. Don't ruin this day for me."

"How could I do that?"

"By going off on some female tirade about my lonely existence, my reclusive nature, my need for someone to share my triumph with. I can feel it coming..."

"Nonsense. I meant it would be even better if Spear Jaguar were buried at the site as well."

"Oh. Yeah, that would be something."

Tam winked and toasted her beer against his, cheerfully covering up a growing ache in her chest and a string of curses to make a sailor blush.

Congratulations, Martin. You're in love with the Ivy League Beast. And it's the last thing in the world he's interested in.

C C C

SinJin clutched the small replica statue, turning it over repeatedly in his hand as he sat on the porch, struggling to concentrate on his notes.

She's avoiding you, asshole.

Maybe he'd ruined it for good. Because he had no doubt at all that Tam had been digging for more than artifacts. She wanted to know, and she had a right to know—but he couldn't answer her question, because he didn't know himself. He hadn't let himself consider it. A girlfriend? Was she actually asking if he wanted a girlfriend? Could she have really meant herself?

Shit. Yes, he wanted more, of course he wanted more! He wanted her to stay. To stay the season. To stay next season. And in between seasons. Because it all made so much more sense with her around, somehow. But she had said she only wanted one night. Maybe a summer fling? No doubt he'd be one in a long series of flings. The girl was the hottest thing in the world, and she knew it, *had to.* He'd look like a fool if he pushed her, asked for more than a couple nights of quick sex.

He was nervous when, hours later, he asked her if she'd like to go to dinner. He had found her in the work hut reviewing her sketches and pouring through his books on Mayan mythology and hieroglyphs. She looked up and took off her glasses.

"What, like a date?" Her disdainful tone made him cringe.

"No, Tam. Like food. Like I don't cook and it's Rosa's night off."

"Oh, okay, then. Because I know you don't *date.*"

"What?"

"Never mind. Give me a chance to shower and change. See you on the porch in a half hour, Professor."

SinJin took his time getting ready, pulling on clothes he rarely wore—expensive slacks and a pressed white linen shirt. He even took the time to shave carefully and rummaged through his drawer for his cologne. *Yes, like a date, damn it.*

When Tam stepped onto the porch, he thought his heart would stop. She wore a white halter dress that showed off her voluptuous figure. He wanted to push her against the wall and take her hard and fast with that dress still on her, and thought of telling her so, just to shock her, but she beat him to it.

"Well, Professor, I have to admit something."

He arched a brow in question and sipped coffee.

"If this were a date, you'd be the most magnificent date I've ever had. Actually, you're probably the most magnificent man I've ever known. But I guess you know that. In any case, I'm sure you don't need compliments from your assistant."

It felt too good, the stroking and flirtation. He scowled.

"That really wasn't an insult, in case you didn't notice. This would be a good time to tell me I look nice, even if it's not a date."

"You look fucking amazing, and you know it. Are you ready to tell me why you're in such a snit over this date business?"

"A snit? You got it wrong, mate. I don't go into snits. I just get really pissed off."

"You know what, Tamara? You talk too much and say too little."

"Asshole. Oops, now I'm fired again. Where are we going for dinner?"

"Just shut up and admire me. Silently."

SinJin drove down the main road towards Akumal, and they stopped at a small, quaint beachside restaurant. He greeted the owner and introduced him to Tam as the brother of their crew chief, Orlando. They were escorted to a private corner of the terrace overlooking a magnificent view of the sea.

Tam sighed as SinJin ordered for them both.

"Now what?"

"You ordered for me again. It's annoying."

"Deal with it."

They sipped wine in awkward silence, both gazing out at the fiery sunset.

He cursed himself for not being able to handle it, for speaking first. "So, is Pacal's curse going to scare you off, Doctor?"

"No, I don't think so. I think you're more likely to do that."

It felt like she hammered a nail into his chest. *So, she would leave. He'd blown it.*

"Perhaps we can start over? I'm sorry about...wait a minute! You started it, didn't you? I was ready for an assistant, and you hit on me."

"Yep, I started it, Professor. Can't blame a girl for trying." She shrugged and smiled a little sadly. "I guess you're the perfect combination of centerfold, prick, and genius. Plus that accent. Couldn't resist. Jack tried to warn me."

"I'm not sure I understand."

"Sure you do. It's okay, I'll get over it. Unrequited sexual crushes haven't killed me yet, and I've had a few, trust me. It won't affect my work, on that you may rely."

She smiled again and tapped her hand on his. He clutched it quickly, heart beating wildly.

No! Oh my God, no. I'm in love with her. He had to stop himself from catching his breath at the sight of her. Not in years had he felt it. *Shit.* He'd simply needed an assistant, then wanted a lover, and perhaps a friend. He looked away to regroup. Why, the last time he felt something like this he had been, God, he ran his hand through his hair, he had been a kid, twenty or so.

"Come on, Professor, lighten up. I'm sorry if I was pissy."

"It's not that."

She tilted her head and examined him closely. "This should be a happy day. What is it? The vandalism? Don't worry, it won't stop us."

"I'm fine, just a little tired, a little anxious to excavate the tomb. Drink up." He pointed to her untouched glass. She picked up her glass and clanked it against his.

"A toast to the Master of Pacal. You've done it, SinJin. You've cemented your reputation for life. Into the history books."

"I have done it, haven't I? It's simply taken four years to find it." He shook his head. To be sharing it with her. It hurt to look at her now. Why was falling in love painful? He thought he'd go insane if he didn't tell her how he felt. How had he let this happen so quickly? It was last night; holding her, kissing her, having her lips all over him. She had responded so perfectly. And having her by his side at the site, sharing his greatest hopes and fears with her, a woman who *understood*. How could he not fall in love with her? The Ivy League Beast had fallen for the beauty. He'd laugh if it didn't hurt so much. They fell back into a painful silence.

"SinJin, about last night..."

"What about it?"

"I can understand you aren't interested in what men disdainfully refer to as a 'relationship,' but a little messing around wouldn't kill us, would it? I really hate you for making me beg like this."

Oh, if you only knew, Tam. I want it all. "I don't get you. You just want to screw around?"

"I've been over last night in my mind a hundred times. Do you remember saying that you're a hopeless tease? It worked. What do you think? It's not like there are dozens of single women hanging out at Cozmano. You said it's been a while, that you get...lonely?"

"I'll take it under advisement."

He was throbbing instantly. His heart was aching, his cock was throbbing, and she was making everything much, much worse. She wanted a meaningless fling. Fine. Well, then, he'd let her have one night. He'd make sure she'd never forget the Beast. And after they made love, he'd tell her how he felt, so she'd leave. Give him back his peace. A girl like that needed to live, he thought, really live. She's young and ambitious and would never isolate herself in his dark, odd world. So he'd lose an assistant. Because she'd know before the night was over that he wanted her more than any woman in the world. He was born wanting her. She'd see right into his heart, he knew it.

Chapter Eight

"Aren't we going home?" Tam tapped her foot nervously as he drove South, instead of towards Cozmano. The silent treatment had lasted through dinner and for the last ten minutes on the road. She wanted to throttle him.

"Come on, Sinj, where are you taking me?" His behavior excited, intrigued, and frightened her. She had seen him flip his cell closed at the restaurant as she returned from the restroom and had assumed he was only checking messages. Had he arranged something? Her heart fluttered. His silence was torture.

Tam tried to concentrate on the scenery, the turquoise water below them, but she couldn't stop herself from sneaking glances at him as he concentrated on the winding road. Just looking at his tanned hands on the steering wheel was pleasurable. He had the most beautiful hands. *Why do you notice things like that when you're falling in love?*

"Dinner was wonderful, thank you very much."

No reaction.

She'd try a new tactic. "Screw you, Professor. Screw you, and your weird moods, and secret agendas." For this, he at least gave her a smirk.

By this point, they were halfway down the coast, close to Pacal. Surely, he wasn't taking her to the site? He finally pulled up a long unmarked drive that opened onto the grounds of an impossibly beautiful resort. "Vista del Mar," Tam read. "Oh, I've heard about this place. Isn't this where the rich and famous stay or something?"

As they left the Land Rover, SinJin threw the keys at a smiling young man.

"Hey SinJin."

"Hey yourself, Tony. How's Marcia?" They chatted for a minute as Tam took in the huge white main house, glistening in the evening light. Fountains and waterfalls graced the elegantly landscaped grounds. It was very peaceful, and Tam could hear the jungle sounds she loved so much.

SinJin didn't speak to her but pushed her abruptly towards the lobby. He grabbed her hand and she felt a rush from the contact. He only slowed briefly to catch a key card in midair, thrown to him by the concierge.

"Someone's a regular. Thought you didn't get out much?"

"You're talking too much again, Doctor."

Tam sniffed in annoyance, wondering about his story of being alone for years. Maybe he had brought many women here. He certainly was acting rather smoothly now. His expensive shoes clicked on the tiles as he pulled her quickly along. Suddenly he seemed more James Bond than Indiana Jones.

They reached the far side of the resort, where a spectacular bungalow nestled amongst the palms and tiny waterfalls. Two floors of marble and glass that peered over the hillside to the gardens and pools below.

"Well, I guess it beats the Holiday Inn. What do they get for this? A couple grand a night?"

"I'm not sure."

"You're not sure?"

He opened the door quickly and ushered her inside. Then he kicked the door behind him and pushed her roughly against the wall, pinning her arms above her head with his strong hands. He stared into her shocked eyes.

"Tonight you're *mine*. No childish protests or pleading. It's too late to change your mind. It's time to put up *and* shut up, Dr. Martin. Is that understood?" His eyes burned as he rubbed his thumb along her bottom lip and unceremoniously caressed one breast through the thin fabric of her dress. Fire danced through her body at his touch, at the smell of his expensive cologne, at the harsh tone of his voice.

"Answer me!"

"What? What am I supposed to say? I've forgotten the question." She heard her own faint whimper as he pinched her nipple and cursed inwardly at how quickly he'd reduced her to jelly.

He simply laughed and turned to pick up the room phone as he kicked his shoes off and unbuttoned his shirt. Placing a rapid-fire room service order in Spanish, he walked to the balcony and threw open the wide doors to reveal a hot tub and plunge pool.

"I suppose we'll be wet soon?" Tam tried to sound nonchalant, but realized with chagrin that she hadn't.

"You're not wet yet?" He winked, taking a chair on the balcony, mostly ignoring her, running his hand through his hair. Finally a rap on the door broke the silence, and SinJin let in a young waiter who was out of breath, obviously having run from the kitchen at full speed to deliver the order. Two bottles of champagne, two glasses, strawberries and whipped cream, chocolates, cakes, and a dozen perfect red roses. SinJin pointed to the balcony and the young man artfully arranged the spread on a table. There were at least a dozen candles on ledges and stands, and the waiter lit each of them. After giving him several bills, SinJin shut the door and walked back onto the balcony.

"Here goes nothing," she muttered.

"What?"

She kicked off her shoes and pulled the pins from her hair, letting it fall to her shoulders. He popped the champagne cork and she stood close as he poured for them both.

"To the beautiful Mistress of Pacal."

"This is rather romantic for you, isn't it? A little out of character?"

"I'm a little rusty, Doctor, but I remember. Or perhaps I'm remembering Cary Grant movies."

"So you fancy yourself suave, debonair?"

"Guardedly optimistic I can at least give that impression."

"You're doing a damned good job."

He placed his glass on the table and peeled his shirt off. Tam's lips were dry and she wanted it to begin. She moved to touch him, and he backed away. Strands of gold-tipped brown hair hung over his brows and she wanted desperately to brush them out of his eyes, hold his face, and kiss him deeply.

"What do you want, Tam?"

"You know what I want, Professor. I want it all. What do you want?"

"Honestly? I want you to take over." He winced and looked a bit uncertain. "So much for suave and debonair, eh?"

"Oh, this is much too nice to be real." She unbuckled his belt and unbuttoned his pants while he sipped champagne and ate a chocolate, watching her breathlessly. Tam turned him to lean on the balcony railing as she pulled his pants to the ground. He stepped out of them and kept his back turned to her.

SinJin groaned as she ran her tongue across his ass, her teeth nipping at him. She worked her way up his back and stood on tiptoes to bite his neck and earlobe, licking his ear.

"I want to you touch yourself, Sinj," she whispered hotly in his ear. He took in a quick breath. "I have to see it again. I'm begging you. And I want you in my mouth."

"What else? Anything."

"I want you to touch me, eat me, lick me, kiss me, everywhere, all night. I want you to fuck the living daylights out of me and never stop. I've never felt like this. I'm afraid I never will again."

He turned to kiss her. She pushed on his chest and backed up. "Not yet." Tam picked up her champagne glass and sat at the table. He was enormous, gorgeous, breathless, perspiring, and barely able to stand. "Tam, please," he begged. "I want to kiss you."

She pointed to his cock and smiled. "You know what I want to see. Please the Mistress of Pacal! Now." He smiled darkly and very slowly, almost shyly, played with his hair with one hand as he squeezed his nipples with the other. He moved his palm down his smooth torso and grabbing his cock, began the slow, long strokes, from one side to the other, over the tip, back and forth, up and down. He moaned lowly as he looked at her from under the hair that had fallen into his eyes. She was mesmerized.

"I'll come soon like this."

"No, not yet."

He groaned and stopped his caresses.

"No, you can't stop. It's not allowed. Just don't come." She grinned and gave him an evil little laugh.

He rubbed himself again. "Tell me what you want. I'll do anything," he gasped out the words.

Tam smiled slowly, watching him approach the brink, then slow down and pull back. He was torturing himself for her. It was exquisite.

"Please, Tam, I can't go on like this."

"Play with your balls for a while, that should slow it down." He winced and cupped himself, gently pulling at the skin and rubbing the base of his cock.

"You are fucking cruel."

"Then beg, Professor."

"Let me come." He grabbed his cock and stroked roughly, quickly. "I'm begging you Tam. I'm dying. Please, please, I'll do anything for you. Anything. Forever."

"Do it now." She moaned as he closed his eyes and tilted his head back. He cried out loudly as he exploded, pouring his release onto his hands, legs shaking, chest heaving.

Tam wanted to cry out with him, but she forced herself to sip nonchalantly from her glass.

"Move the candles around the tub. I need more light." He looked startled, barely recovered from his orgasm. He slowly began to rearrange things. She pointed to the hot tub, and he climbed in. Tam brought him his glass and some sweets on a plate, and told him to drink, then took a seat across from him. She pinched her nipples through the silken fabric of her dress. Then she pulled the skirt up enough to slip her hand underneath and brush her soaked pussy. She brought her fingers to her lips, rubbed the wetness on them, and puckered a kiss at him.

"You are so *not* fired," he said, making her laugh despite her efforts to be serious. She unfastened the halter dress and let it slide to the ground. And watched.

He groaned loudly. "God damn. Bare. I..."

"You like?"

"Oh, Doctor, you're a living, breathing fantasy."

She spread her legs, propping her high heels on the edge of the pool.

"You're a goddess. The Mistress of Pacal is full of surprises."

"Good surprises?"

"Oh, very, very good ones."

She pinched her hard nipples with one hand and brought the other down to her pussy as she spoke. "You asked me what I do, remember?" He shook his head slowly in acknowledgment. "I do it all. Everything you can imagine, and some things you haven't thought of. And I do them all the time. And yes, I do them under your roof." She slid three fingers inside herself and he could see every detail as she fucked herself with them, moaning and arching. She never stopped looking into his eyes. Without stopping, she rubbed her clit with her other hand, back and forth until she exploded in wave after wave of release. She gradually came back to consciousness and looked at him.

"Your mouth is hanging open, sailor." She smiled.

"I suppose it is. Damn, you could make a lot of money doing that in front of a camera." She laughed and he laughed with her. She slid into the tub and sat next to him, sipping from his champagne glass. She could see that he was as hard as a rock again, and she knew they were just beginning the night.

"You know, you *have* ruined me for other men. Isn't that what you wanted?"

"Part of what I want. And to think, I haven't even touched you yet." He leaned over and kissed her and she moaned. He was tender, loving, perfect. And then he held her head and changed the kiss and brought all the passion back to the night. She reached under the water, found his cock, and grabbed it hard. His kiss became desperate as she stroked him. He filled his hands with her breasts and rubbed them gently and then fiercely, squeezing her nipples while he bit at her lips and neck.

"Say your prayers, dear, we're going to bed." He lifted her out of the water, carried her over his shoulder to the room, and dumped her soaking wet onto the bed. He grabbed a towel, brushed her down quickly, and dried himself off. Then he knelt next to the bed and examined his prize. Tam was incredibly frustrated. Surely, he wouldn't leave her again?

"Tam. I'm going to make you come now, and I pray you think I'm the best, because I need that, desperately. I'm frustrated that I care so much. And then I'm going to fuck you so hard you won't know what hit you."

"Do you always tell somebody what you're going to do before you do it?"

"No, never. As I was saying before I was rudely interrupted," he smiled, "I'm going to suck on that gorgeous bare pussy of yours until you beg me to fuck you. But before I do," he hesitated, lowering his forehead into his hands, "I want to ask you a favor."

"A favor?"

"Stay."

"Stay?"

"Yes. With me. Don't go home. Do you understand? But, if this has to be the last time we're together, if you decide to leave tomorrow, well, I'll understand. I mean, you came to work, not to find a..."

"Lover?" She smiled.

He nodded.

"Sinj, as long as we're playing true confessions, here, I may as well tell you something. And I have the feeling I'll regret it, and I don't want to lose my job again." He laughed.

Was he ready? It didn't matter. Roll the dice and live with the consequences. Because you won't be able to stay with him as a friend or colleague. It would never be enough, and the pain would become unbearable.

"Professor, I've gone and done the unthinkable."

"Oh Lord, what's that?"

"I've started to fall in love with you."

"Could you repeat that?"

"I'm falling in love with you." She looked at him seriously now, worried. He looked so stunned. He had wanted a lover, he had wanted her, but not this. How stupid—he must think her a naïve child. Of course, how many women had said that to him, thrown themselves at him? Humiliated, she turned away and began to climb off the other side of the huge bed.

"Where the hell do you think you're going?" He was yelling.

"Leave me alone."

"Tam, come here."

She walked towards the bathroom. SinJin caught up with her and grabbed her arm, swinging her around to face him, tilting her chin up to drill into her eyes with his.

Then he pulled her into his body and held her so tightly she thought he would crush her.

"You mean it!"

"Leave me alone," she mumbled into his chest.

"Not a chance, Dr. Martin, not a chance. Not ever. Didn't you hear me before? I asked you to *stay*." And there it was in his voice, what she had longed to hear. She hesitated and looked up at him to find him grinning at her. "I guess I'm not that great with words."

"Oh."

"Right. You said you wanted a lover, didn't you? All right, you have one." He laughed and threw her onto the bed. "Now, back to that conversation we were having. What was it I was going to do to you? I forgot?"

"Are you sure you want me to stay? I mean, with you, not only at the site?"

"For God's sake, Tam. If I tell you I'm falling in love with you, will that shut you up?"

"Oh my God. Oh my God, Sinj. Say it again."

"No way. You heard me. You'll have to trust your memory. Don't push it, Doctor."

He held her arms down and stared into her eyes. Then he brought his mouth down on hers and pulled her apart with his hot lips, his tongue, his teeth. Tam wanted to hold him but was overwhelmed with the sensations he created. He moved to her breasts and sucked on her nipples, sending flames through her body. She groaned his name. He licked his way to her pussy and brought his hot tongue onto her clit. Tam cried out as he licked her up and down, sucked and nibbled. He brought her to the edge and then pulled back, returning to her breasts and her mouth.

"See, Doctor. Not so nice to be tortured like that, is it?"

"Oh, Professor. It's so very nice."

He took her clit into his mouth and sucked as he pushed his fingers into her dripping folds. She let go and he watched the blush of her ecstasy wash up her body. Tam grabbed his hair and rode his hand, crying his name.

"I can't wait, Tam, I have to have you now."

"Please, now, oh yes."

He thrust into her quickly, with one hard push that brought a scream from her and a loud groan from him.

"I'm sorry, that was too quick. It's been so long..."

"Would you shut up and fuck me, SinJin? You're perfect." Tam felt tears of passion build as she squeezed at his cock, clutched at his back, craving to meld her body and soul with his. *He wants me.*

"Oh, damn, you are fucking incredible." He began to move slowly at first, long deep strokes that filled her completely. She was on fire and matched his rhythm. "Oh God help me." He slid in and out and quickly lost control, slamming into her, yelling her name as he came, as she came. They held each other, throbbing, for minutes. Tam could feel his quick heartbeat and breathing against her cheek as she nestled against his chest. It matched her own.

"Tam. Damn."

"Yeah, I know. God almighty."

He propped himself up on one arm and smiled at her.

"What the hell happened to the Beast? You're grinning like a fool."

"Oh, he's still in there. I'm sorry that was so fast. Guess I needed to get that one out of my system. Wanna try again?"

He held her tightly and kissed her hair, stroked her back.

"Oh yes, I do. But just hold me for a minute. Damn, that sounds lame. Sorry, Professor."

"Actually, this is almost as good as sex, and I'm the last person I expected to hear say that." He pulled her tighter and she quickly brushed away a tear that slipped out.

"I don't know anything about you, Tam."

"Sure you do. I read glyphs and you love having sex with me. Can't imagine you'd care about more than that."

"You're wrong. Well, I don't really care, but what if someone asks me something about my new 'lover'? I should be able to have something to tell them."

She tapped him lightly on the cheek. "Asshole."

"Go ahead, tell me anything. Favorite color. Where were you born?"

"Green. And I'm originally from Canterbury, but was raised in Manhattan."

"How romantic."

"Not really. We also lived in Boston. My parents are the retired Professors Martin, astrophysicists. Only child."

He nonchalantly played with her breasts. "Your father is George Martin? I lived in a dorm at Harvard named after him. Ah, the daughter of a legend. Wait, your mother is too, right?"

Tam laughed. "Yeah, I'm the offspring of a couple of geeks. And somehow, they're still proud of me. Maybe I'm a geek and I don't know it?"

"Yeah, you're a real geek with that sharp tongue and stripper's body. Maybe you were adopted?"

"Come on, Professor, tell me about yourself." Tam looked deeply into his eyes and rubbed her hand along his muscular arm, bit back a sigh.

"I've already told you more than I've ever told anyone. No, seriously. I have a sister, Cynthia. She lives close by. You'll love her, and she'll *adore* you. And of course, she'll tell you anything you want to know. She's the insane one."

"And you are filthy stinking rich, am I right? You try to hide it, but it shows anyway."

"Hmm. Well, Dad did have a pretty good business sense, yes."

"So you don't have to worry about funding from Princeton or the University of Mexico, or anywhere else? Wow. Most guys with your looks and your money would, you know, go yachting or something?"

"You really like the way I look?"

"Shut up. I'm not going to feed your ego."

"Please? Anyway, you know me better than you think. Because, deep down, we have to be the same sort of person to be passionate about a secondary Post Classic site, don't we?"

"Yes, I suppose you're right."

"And then, there's this." He brought his hand between her thighs and started circling her clit with his thumb. He leaned in and kissed her thoroughly, beautifully. As she groaned his name, he caught it with his kiss.

"Take over, Dr. Martin."

"I love it when you tell me to take over."

"I know. I do too."

☾ ☾ ☾

"Oooh, husband, I liked that part."

Shield Jaguar snickered and set his cup on the floor, rolled A'ok onto her back, and leaned in to kiss her sweet lips. "And would you prefer to be with the storyteller, or with your husband?"

"Ah, you are my Lord. But perhaps you wouldn't mind if I pretend that the storyteller is with us now?"

"Should I pretend that the female storyteller is also here?" Shield Jaguar pressed his cock against her mound and she reached down to guide him into her, then laced her fingers in his long black hair.

"I care not, Lord. I only care that you take me."

"You don't care if I want another?"

"You want no other. You want A'ok. You love her. Please, Lord, tell me."

Shield Jaguar ignored her plea, fighting his heart, silently begging for her to proclaim her love for him first. It is the way it must be, he thought. I am Lord.

☾ ☾ ☾

"Don't look so pissed. I can't help it, Ramirez will be there today." SinJin pushed Tam into the Land Rover and she snarled at him. "Growl all you want, I know you're smiling inside."

"Smug bastard. I'm not pissed, just disappointed we can't stay longer."

He smiled. "Me, too, Doctor, trust me." *If you only knew. Longer? I want longer to be forever. Geez, SinJin, what have you gotten yourself into?*

Rosa waited for them on the porch, hands on her hips, looking very disapproving.

"I sent my cousin, Orlando, to look for you at the site! You could have left me a note, SinJin Twaine. You are not too old to put over my knee. Well, perhaps a little old for that. But do not make Rosa worry so!"

"Hello, Rosa. I'm sorry, Mama. I should have left you a note, you're right." SinJin kissed her on the forehead and walked past her into his bedroom, shutting the door.

"Yes, you should have," she yelled after him.

He peeked out his window onto the porch, amused as the women faced off.

"Are you okay, Miss?" Rosa frowned at Tam, and then her frown gradually grew into a knowing grin.

"Oh, Rosa, you know I am." Tam laughed and hugged her. Rosa clapped her hands in glee and did a little dance on the porch. Tam laughed harder.

Rosa leaned to Tam and whispered. "Miss, was it good? Was it very, very good?"

"Rosa, if he weren't like a son to you, I'd tell you how good it was." She winked.

"Oh, tell me anyway!"

SinJin drew the curtains aside. "I can *hear* you!"

Rosa fell into fits of laughter, and Tam stormed off to her room.

When SinJin knocked quickly and opened Tam's door minutes later, he found her sound asleep on her bed, still fully dressed. He was about to wake her with a growl and stopped himself. What would it hurt to give her some rest? He had worn her out, he thought smugly.

He told Rosa to let Tam sleep, quickly grabbed coffee and a roll, and started to the Land Rover. Rosa ran after him. "Can you take me to the market? I can take the bus back, but I need a few things for dinner."

"Of course. If you want, spend the day in town and I'll pick you up at lunchtime? Actually, there's something I need to do in Playa if you don't mind going there?" A whim turned into an obsession. He'd laid awake, wondering if there were a chance... Well, if he bought the ring, it didn't mean he had to ask her right away. She'd stay on the site, and when the time was right, in weeks or in months, he'd know it. Rosa chatted excitedly as SinJin sped down the road to Playa del Carmen, whistling happily, leaving Tam to her dreams. He wondered if she'd dream of him, then felt foolish for being so in love.

Chapter Nine

Tam thought she was dreaming at first, but then he repeated the order, and she knew the gun at her temple was very real. He was tall, quite handsome, and obviously Mexican, although he spoke fluent, nearly unaccented English. A dead ringer for Antonio Banderas, Tam thought numbly. Alberto Ramirez, the head of Mexican Antiquities, holding a pistol to her skull. Her body felt like it was melting off her bones. She had never known true terror before, she realized. Everything felt as if it were happening in slow motion.

"Who are you? Why are you here?" She moved to wipe away her tears and he waved the gun in her face.

"No movements. No questions, or he will die. You will follow my orders exactly, Dr. Martin. Understood?" Tam nodded, her mind racing. Wasn't this man SinJin's friend? In fact, wasn't he his new boss? She couldn't take it in. He must be mad. A madman was holding a gun to her head.

"Get up, not a word. Pack your things, quickly. Every last item, do you understand?"

"No, I don't understand."

Ramirez slapped her and she fell back onto the bed. Her cheek throbbed and she began sobbing.

"Shut up! Shut up! Do what I say."

She nodded and started pushing clothes and toiletries into her suitcase. He pointed to items he recognized must be hers and she numbly, methodically scooped them up. Ramirez circled the room, opening drawers and the closet, satisfying himself that she had left nothing behind.

Tam desperately tried to pull herself together, fearing for SinJin as much as herself. *Think, Tam, think.* Her heart was breaking. It was impossible. *I just found the man of my dreams and my life is going to end. And perhaps SinJin's?*

"Now, paper and a pen." She opened the desk, drew out a fresh notebook, and flattened it open.

"Sit. Write a note to your beloved Professor. A love letter, my dear. I had the great honor to witness a bit of your little night of passion. So fill it with heartfelt regret. You can't go on; you aren't ready, blah, blah, blah."

He squatted next to her and hissed into her ear as he held the gun to the back of her head. "No tricks, I'll spot them. And you'll both die."

Tam began crying, not able to write a word, not able to lift the pen. How could she warn SinJin? Tam heard Ramirez release the gun's safety, and sucking in a tearful breath, picked up the pen. For him, she thought. I'll hurt his feelings but save his life. At least she hoped was saving him. She wrote as her tears plopped onto the page with each sentence.

C C C

Rosa smiled at SinJin as he whistled happily.

"So, you and Tamara?"

"Hmm."

"Oh, come on, son. Talk to Rosa."

He laughed. "Mamacita, I'm going to ask her to marry me. Maybe not right away, but soon. I'm going to get hitched."

"Hitched? Married!" She erupted into a flood of excited Spanish. "Are you sure? Is she sure? Oh, SinJin, no, it's too soon! What are you thinking?"

He looked at her seriously, seeing how stunned she was.

"Who is this man before me? The handsome loner I think of as a son? What have you done with that man?"

SinJin laughed lightly. He did feel reborn.

"I've watched you work your fingers to the bone, watched you bury your parents, your wife, the baby. SinJin, I've watched you bury yourself. How has this girl changed that dead man?"

"Dead?" A flare of anger rose up, but the ring of truth in her words made him bite back a retort. *Dead. You did bury something, SinJin.*

"Well, I've haven't asked her yet. Don't worry, Rosa, I know what I'm doing. In a month or two, maybe."

"Dios mio! You mean to ask her right away, it's written across that handsome face! Well, all I can do is wish you luck."

"Do you like her, Rosa? Be truthful."

"I like her. I like her very much. But that does not matter. It matters only that you love one another. Only time will tell, eh? You are putting the cart before the horse, as they say. But sometimes the horse manages to move the cart from behind anyway."

Rosa squirmed close to plant a big kiss on his cheek.

"You're going to help me pick out an engagement ring today. But keep it a secret—I don't know how this is going to turn out. I'm getting prepared, you understand?"

She clapped her hands in excitement. "I do love to shop! How about the work? Who will go to the site today?"

"Oh, I'll go later. Orlando can handle things until I arrive. I knew I was going to take her to the resort yesterday. I told Orlando's brother to let him know we might be rather late."

"You took her to Villa del Mar? How will you ever top that for your honeymoon?"

"I'll have a lot of fun trying."

They reached Playa del Carmen too early for the shops to be open, and SinJin treated Rosa to a luxurious breakfast at one of the resorts. He had trouble keeping up a conversation. His mind wandered back to the night, to Tam, to the next time he would be with her.

"Oh my, boss, you are with her in your head."

"It shows? God, how embarrassing."

"It's a good sign." She sighed. "Ah, I remember a time when I was so in love. Look, the shops are opening. Where will you buy the ring?"

They entered the most exclusive shop in the town. The jeweler, an older man in a perfectly tailored suit, greeted SinJin cordially. SinJin saw him glance at his watch, a high-end piece, and knew the man probably had him pegged as the eccentric billionaire from Cozmano in an instant.

"And what kind of ring were you considering?"

"Only one. It's in the window." SinJin saw the hopeful gleam in the salesman's eye and followed him to the window, where he pointed to the treasure. The salesman was nearly salivating. Rosa gasped.

"What do you think?" SinJin turned to the matron.

"I think that Tamara Martin is the luckiest woman in the world, for more reasons than one. And I think if you can afford that ring, I need to ask for a raise."

"Done," he leaned down and kissed her. She giggled and clapped her hands. "This is all too fantastic!"

It wasn't that the diamond was big, which it was. And not that it was set in an exquisite platinum band littered with smaller stones. But it was pure, perfect, and radiant.

"Rare, sir. I do not just talk the pitch now, you understand? You see the pink, no?" He handed SinJin a loop.

"It doesn't matter. She stared at it the other day as if it were a gorgeous sunset."

The salesman took a deep breath. "Three hundred thousand, American."

SinJin reached into his backpack and pulled out his banker's business card, his checkbook, and his passport, handing all three to the salesman, who looked at him reverently. He returned moments later from speaking with SinJin's banker and smiled.

Rosa and SinJin glanced at the cases while the salesman wrapped the ring.

"And these for you, Rosa." He pointed to ruby earrings, kissing Rosa's cheek as she squealed. The salesman rushed over and pulled the earrings from the case. He handed them to Rosa, who put them on immediately.

Then he held up the necklace that had caught SinJin's attention. Several gold strands laced with exquisite emeralds. SinJin nodded and the salesman looked as if he would faint.

"She's supposed to get a wedding gift, right?" SinJin asked Rosa.

Rosa shook her head in amazement. "SinJin," she spoke softly, not wanting the jeweler to hear, "Don't you think you need to propose to her before you buy her a wedding gift? Have you considered, well, you know?"

"Don't even say it. She'll accept. She has to."

After Rosa's run through the grocery store, they made their way back to Cozmano. Today he had to pay attention to his other mistress, Pacal. He had neglected the site, and it was calling his name, whispering to him. Ramirez would be either at the site or waiting for him at Cozmano. Perhaps he had met Tam. But he wanted Tam with him when he broke through the inner wall of Shield Jaguar's tomb. Today, today they would have their prize. God willing, the tomb would be intact, untouched by grave robbers, ancient or modern.

SinJin had hoped Tam would be on the porch, waiting for him. He had missed her after only a few hours, he thought in wonder. She must be still asleep. He pushed open her door.

"All right, Dr. Sleepyhead." He froze. Rosa joined him and gasped.

Gone.

Not a single piece of clothing. Not a shoe, piece of jewelry, bottle of suntan lotion.

And on the desk, a notebook, opened. A pen lay across the page. SinJin walked to the desk as if in a dream. There would be an explanation. She had gone shopping, checked into Vista del Mar as a surprise, hitched a ride to the site.

He looked at the perfect writing, smeared in places from what must have been her tears.

"Dear Beast,

I don't know how to say this, and I know you'll never forgive me. I don't expect you to. I have to leave. I care very much about you, and last night was wonderful—you are wonderful. But I've thought it over. I can't stay with you. I'm so sorry. I've gone to stay with my brother in Europe, so don't come looking for me at Princeton, you won't find me there. I know you won't believe this, but I do care for you, and I wish I were a different sort of person, one who could be happy at Cozmano, at Pacal. There's someone else I need to work things out with. I pray you'll understand.

Tam

PS. Regards to Shield Jaguar."

Impossible. The bag of gifts fell from his hand to the floor. Rosa moved to the notebook. She brought her hand to her mouth as she read it, and tears filled her eyes. She looked at SinJin, who brushed away a single tear in embarrassment.

"Go after, her, SinJin, find her. She can't have gone far. She has to leave from Cancun. Go, hurry."

He walked from the room, and the house, wondering where to go. He had to escape the pain in his chest. SinJin tore down the road, not thinking, not feeling. He reached the deserted beach and strode to the water. He kicked off his flip-flops, pulled off his shirt, and dove in. If he closed his eyes and floated, he couldn't really feel his body, which was a good thing. The sky was cloudless, as it usually was on a Mayan morning, he thought. The workmen would be at the site, and Ramirez would be looking for him. He would show up soon. Pacal was his, and Shield Jaguar's tomb would be his as well. It was all he needed.

The salt water stung his back a bit and he wondered what he had done to himself. *Don't think about it. You dreamt her.* But the living proof was there. She had scratched his back raw in places, moaning her desire for him, screaming for him, begging him to be hers. You stupid son of a bitch, he thought. It didn't matter. He had Pacal, he repeated to himself again and again. He didn't need anything else. But the lie hurt as badly as the loss of her. She had even taken Pacal away from him. It meant next to nothing now. The mistress of Pacal was gone.

ᑕ ᑕ ᑕ

It was getting worse by the minute. Tam didn't know where Ramirez was taking her, but it was close to the site and far from the resort areas. Tam thought of trying to get the car door open and running for it, but with her hands tied, he'd be on her in a second. *SinJin, where are you?* She had to find out what was going on, reason with him. Reason with a madman.

"I don't understand why you're doing this. What has he done to you? What do you want?"

He ignored her, maneuvering down the bumpy back road and speaking softly to himself.

Then she saw the hut and knew they had reached her prison. She prayed it would be a prison rather than a tomb. He pulled her roughly into the dark, long-abandoned thatched-roof hut, once a shelter from the sun for local laborers. It smelled foul.

"Please, Professor, I'll do whatever you want. Please don't hurt me, don't hurt him."

"My dear, I need you alive, as insurance, you understand. But only for a few days. If Twaine doesn't operate as I expect him to, then, you will both have to die." He was completely matter-of-fact, and Tam knew he had lost all sense of conscience. He would kill them if he had to. But why?

"Have you been warning us away from the site? Whispering to us while we work?"

"Don't be ridiculous! Why would I stoop to childish pranks?"

"And the blood? Was that you?"

"Blood! What is going on at Pacal! I received an odd message from Twaine about vandalism, but there was no mention of blood!"

"Someone poured blood, gallons of it, on the pyramid."

He swore in Spanish, and she was convinced it was the first he had heard of it. He was tying her to a post that supported the roof and was about to gag her.

"Please. I have the right to know why I'm going to die. What do you want?"

He slapped her and she nearly fainted from the pain. "Is that enough of an answer?" She was terrified and furious. She spat out the blood from her cut inner cheek.

"Now, you have one chance to live through this day, do you understand me?" Tam nodded. "Tell me everything you know about the tomb. The location of the entrance, why he is convinced it is Shield Jaguar, everything."

"The tomb? I don't understand. SinJin was going to show you the tomb as soon as you arrived."

"Finders-keepers you Americans say, no? SinJin opens the tomb in front of many witnesses; does it not become SinJin's great achievement? I have allowed Twaine to do my work for a number of years, knowing he has the talent, well, gift actually, for sniffing out the most important finds. But nothing has been this important, this priceless. Coupled with a few recent indiscretions, shall we say, at the university, I will need this discovery to keep my position. This will mark me in the annals of archaeology for all time. Understand?"

"Why not just fire SinJin, or take the site from him? Kick him out—aren't you in charge of all antiquities?"

"Politics, my dear. American universities, American funds, much of it SinJin's funds. Do you think that all of this work can be done by my institution? We are hanging on by a thread. And the Government will not allow us to offend our rich northern neighbors, of course." He spat. "And I know SinJin. I saw it. He will brood over you, lose himself for days, in drink perhaps. He will lose his love of Pacal, perhaps even pack up. If that doesn't work," he shrugged, "I'll kill him. I wouldn't mind having him here now, actually." Tam saw a dark look cross his face. "Your Professor Twaine, so handsome, no?" He touched her cheek with the gun barrel and a chill ran through her. "Am I not as handsome?" He laughed as he saw her revulsion. "Don't worry, dear, you aren't my type. Now SinJin, that's another story." Tam gasped, and he laughed. "It wasn't you I was looking at last night on that grand balcony, Dr. Martin, trust me. But alas, our dear Professor has made it perfectly clear to me on several occasions that I am most definitely not his type. So you see, you are safe with me. Well, of course I'll kill you, but I won't rape you." He leaned in, and she smelled his expensive cologne. "Tell me, Dr. Martin. What was it like? What did he do to you? Describe it, describe him, in detail, my dear. I want the dirty little secrets. What does my friend like to do in the dark of the night? Who was in charge? He likes to be in charge, doesn't he? Doesn't he?" Ramirez pushed the gun under her chin.

Tears flowed down Tam's face. How could she do this? She wouldn't recount the truth. That was all she had of SinJin, her memories of their few days together, of their passion. She would lie. Tam began an erotic tale she thought this man would like, full of sexual darkness and brutality. It was not close to the truth, but she saw his eyes burn. She nearly vomited when she saw him unclasp his belt.

☾ ☾ ☾

Rosa paced, desperately seeking an answer. It was not right, she knew it. Tam had been ecstatic today, falling in love. Impossible that she had changed her mind in a few hours. Rosa had seen into her heart, the heart of a woman who was so happy she could barely think. Something, or someone, had convinced her to leave. The curse of Pacal? No, a Mayan ghost hadn't written that letter. She rifled through SinJin's room, searching desperately for the notebook of contacts he kept. What was his name, that boy that Tam knew? *Come on, Rosa, think!* Peders! There it was. She picked up SinJin's phone from the desk and dialed. It was a long shot, but perhaps he would know something.

"Hello?"

"Señor Peders?"

"What's happened? Is it about Tam Martin? Who is this?"

"Jack, listen. It is Rosa, Professor Twaine's housekeeper. Do you remember me? Tamara is not hurt, everything is fine. Well, not really fine." She began to cry and tried to explain what had happened. It sounded unreal to her as she tried to convince him that Tamara was in love with SinJin.

"Look, Rosa, I can't understand why you'd lie to me about something like this, but it doesn't make sense. She's only been there a few days!"

"I know, I know, Jack. Listen, all I want to know is whether she called. You are good friends, correct? She might ask you to pick her up at the airport, something like that? She wrote that she was going to stay with her brother in Europe, but I thought she would have to return to Princeton first?"

"Her brother in Europe? She doesn't have a brother, Rosa." Now Jack sounded worried. "Are you sure that's what she wrote?" Rosa read the letter to him.

"Listen, Jack, I know that this sounds ridiculous to you, but I believe someone convinced her to leave SinJin. It is the only way she would have gone. She was very, very happy hours before. You must trust me on this. Now I am very worried someone might have taken her."

"Taken her! But why?"

"Because of the site? There have been vandals, and then, of course, the site has the problem."

"Oh, don't start that curse talk. Listen, I want you to call the police right away, do you hear me? I'm going to get a hold of her parents, and then I'll fly down as soon as I can. Tonight if I can make it. Tell the police that you think she left a note giving false information as a clue that she has been taken. Do you understand me Rosa? Repeat everything I said." Rosa had it nailed down.

"And Rosa? Where is the Professor? Is he looking for her?"

"No, you see Jack that is the problem. He has gone away for a while, because, well, his heart is broken, you understand?"

"The Beast is off nursing a broken heart?"

"Oh yes, he most certainly is."

Chapter Ten

"Come to me. Hurry."

SinJin woke in a sweat from another nightmare of death at Pacal to hear the urgent whisperings on the breeze. It must have been part of the dream, and the dream was from the tequila, he thought, disgusted with himself. He couldn't even get drunk. His plan to climb into a bottle for a few days had fizzled out. SinJin had lost interest halfway through the bender and plunged headfirst into indulgent grief and self-pity, rehearsing every moment he had spent with Tam. The way she arched her back on the beach, teasing him. Their flirting. Talking about the site, working side by side. Her hair brushing her cheek. Holding her. Kissing her.

"No, Professor, we have not cleaned it yet!" The concierge protested as SinJin had headed back to the room at Vista del Mar. He wanted it as they had left it. Exactly as they had left it. An inch of flat champagne in the glasses. Roses fully opened now, chocolates melting in the morning sun. He crawled into the bed and felt her presence. It was still there, still with him. Her scent on the pillow, on the sheet, on his soul. A towel on the floor from her shower. A blonde hair caught in the brush. He pulled it out gently and let it flutter on the breeze blowing in from the balcony. He *hadn't* imagined the night. He gripped the tiny statue she had given him, and threw it against the wall, where it crumbled into tiny bits of clay.

"Hurry, I need you. Come to Pacal!"

His heart beat wildly. Was he losing his mind? The voice of the King, the voice of Pacal, Shield Jaguar? Tam had heard it too, at the site. A warning. But hadn't they been warnings to leave the site? Weren't the warnings from an angry King who wanted his tomb to remain undisturbed for eternity? Or had the King been warning him of danger all along?

Ridiculous. He might actually be insane. What did it matter? The damage had been done already, so what help were warnings now?

The phone jarred him out of his self-pity. "Sí?"

"SinJin, it is Rosa."

"Rosa, what's wrong?" He could tell she was crying.

"I hoped to find you there. I believe, well, I know, that something is very wrong."

"What do you mean?"

"I called Jack Peders—the boy, you remember, Tam's friend? I wondered if she had called him." SinJin groaned in annoyance. He didn't want the world to know he was dumped and pining.

"No, listen. Jack said that Tam does not have a brother, could not be going to Europe."

"Well, she made up a stupid story, then," he said uncertainly, remembering that she had said she was an only child.

"Listen, SinJin, how long have I known you? Your pain blinds you now. I can see clearly. You must trust me, trust my female instincts. Something is very, very wrong. Tam is in love with you. She was the happiest woman alive, and may the Virgin Mother, herself, appear to me at this moment if I am not correct. Tam did not leave you. Someone took her, I am sure. I think that she tried to tell you, by writing of a brother she does not have. Jack agrees with me, and he knows her best. Do you hear me, SinJin? I believe she is in very bad trouble."

"Hurry!"

"I'm coming home, Rosa. Have you called the police?"

"Oh yes, they said it was too soon, and that she left a note saying what she was doing. Lover's quarrel, they called it. They would not listen, do you understand SinJin? We must find her."

"If she didn't leave me, then we'll find her."

"She didn't leave you, SinJin."

☾ ☾ ☾

Exhaustion swept over Tam. Ramirez had gagged her and left her alone in the dark heat. He had grilled her for two hours on SinJin, on the site, on the tomb. She had done her best to lie, putting enough truth in to make it believable and enough falsehood to keep her treasured memories private. Tam had held back some of what she knew of Shield Jaguar, managing to place a bit of doubt in Ramirez's mind about the occupant of the tomb. But it all seemed pretty useless. He would kill her. No one knew where she was, and SinJin had probably believed the note. That was the worst part.

He would think she had betrayed him. Perhaps he'd never learn what had happened. She would die a few miles from Cozmano, less than a mile from the site, and he'd work there for years, thinking she was living her life in Europe. It would crush her parents. Tam cried herself to a fitful sleep and dreamt of a sleek cat standing atop a pyramid, gazing down at her. She woke with a start.

"Do not give up. I am here."

The whisper came on a breeze through the small window of the hut, and Tam dismissed it as part of her nightmare. She had already given up. No one was going to rescue her. She would not spend her life with SinJin. Hope had slipped away.

C C C

Orlando regarded the tall handsome man curiously. He had seen him once, briefly, and knew that he was who he claimed to be. Alberto Ramirez, the head of the Mexican archaeological service. Ramirez had dismissed the workers, all but Orlando. Orlando had questioned him, but had not gotten an answer until they were alone.

"Now, Señor, it is time for my guided tour of Pacal. I want to explore the site fully, especially the tomb opening, and I do not want the entire crew to be here. There has been vandalism, and one of them is to blame. Tomb robbing will be next."

"No! I can vouch for each man. In fact, I'm related to nearly all of them in some way. You are wrong, Señor." He saw the flash of temper in Ramirez's eyes. "I mean no offense."

"Well, it is still best this way. Show me the tomb."

"I do not understand why you do not want Professor Twaine to show you the tomb? He is only a few miles away. We can reach him easily. He would want to be here, certainly."

"Orlando, is it? I am in charge of all the archaeological sites in this country. Arc you aware of that?" He was practically hissing. "Twaine is in charge of nothing. Nothing! Is that understood? I strongly urge you to follow my directions."

Orlando nodded obediently, realizing that something was very, very wrong. The man seemed possessed. Orlando had seen a similar look in Twaine's eyes before, but SinJin had always shown restraint and proceeded calmly and kindly, no matter what urgency he felt. Orlando would take the risk. SinJin was a friend, if a gruff one. This man was not SinJin's friend, and he seemed indeed to be his enemy.

"All right, Señor. Come with me and I will show you the place." Orlando led Ramirez to the far side of the pyramid, where a tumble of foundations framed a small opening. Ramirez grunted, squatting to examine the glyphs on the slabs. He ran his hand over them and read the ones that were legible.

"Ah, Orlando, you have made a grave error. Here there are references to Shield Jaguar's son. This would never be enough to convince Twaine that the father is buried at the site. You are holding back on me."

Ramirez's eyes burned into him as he drew a gun. Orlando felt his blood turn to ice and backed up, tripping on a chunk of foundation.

"Now, Orlando. You have one, I repeat, one chance to undo that mistake. If you try to mislead me again, I will maim you. Then you will be truthful. Now, what's the point in that?"

Orlando realized he was a dead man in any case. Ramirez wouldn't leave him alive to talk. He made a break for the jungle and heard the shot long before he felt it. His world spun away as he hit the jungle floor, and the last thing he heard was Ramirez's curse.

Ramirez kicked at Orlando, who seemed unconscious and barely alive. He might still need him to find the tomb, but he'd be sure to kill him before leaving.

Then Ramirez heard the Land Rover. Well, he had badly miscalculated the girl's affect on SinJin. He was back at the site, ready for work, evidently. It might be best, he thought. The boy genius would show him the tomb. In fact, wasn't that what SinJin had been waiting to do for days? Ramirez smiled and waited for his old friend. He would be happy to see him.

He lost his smile when he saw SinJin's face—anger, anguish, anxiety. He'd have to think on his feet. It was falling apart. He hadn't really wanted to kill him, but it might come to that quickly. Ramirez knew SinJin always carried a gun in the jungle.

"Well, my old friend," Ramirez offered his hand, "Here I am at last."

"Where is everyone?" SinJin patted his colleague on the back when he released his hand.

"Oh, I couldn't find you. Your crew chief, what is his name?"

"Orlando."

"Orlando, yes. He told me you might not make it today. So I sent them home, not sure what you intended for them. By the way, buddy, you look terrible."

"It's, well, it's about a girl. I've been seeing someone. Actually, she's my assistant, and she seems to be missing."

"Missing? She was here about an hour ago! Gorgeous blonde? Dr. Martin, that's it. Dressed a little inappropriately for the site, I thought." He laughed lightly and took in SinJin's amazed expression. "She seems rather nice, Twaine. What's the problem?"

"What was she doing here alone? How did she get here? What did she say?"

"Oh, she wasn't alone. She had evidently gone for a walk and one of the workers saw her and gave her a lift. She said she wanted to see you, I suppose she expected to find you here."

"That doesn't make sense. Her bag was gone. You said that she was in a dress? A white dress? Why would she go for a walk with her suitcase? No, Alberto, something's very wrong. It's not adding up. No one seemed to force her to get into the truck? She didn't seem frightened?"

"Not from what I saw, man." Ramirez laughed again. "Very lovely girl. She did mutter something about needing to think and going away and then having changed her mind. All very romantic stuff. Seems like you two have a stormy relationship going on. Don't worry, SinJin, no doubt she's tucked safely away at Cozmano."

"I just came from Cozmano. I didn't pass the men on the road. Unless she asked to go somewhere else, asked them to take her to the bus station in Playa."

"No, she intended to see you back home, no doubt about it. Seemed pretty smitten to me. They probably took the back roads to drop off some of the crew. Don't worry." Ramirez grew impatient with SinJin's obsession with the girl. This was getting him nowhere quickly.

SinJin ran his hand through his hair. "I'm going home, I have to see her."

"Look, Twaine, I know you're anxious for the reunion, but I'm only here for an hour. I've been waiting most of the day and I have to get all the way to Merida tonight. If we're going to look at this tomb, it has to be now. I can't get back down for another two weeks, at least. At least let's make sure it's intact."

SinJin sighed. He felt ill, thinking that she might be waiting for him. He looked at Ramirez, knowing that he couldn't put off the man like this—he'd never get the permit for the full excavation if he did.

"Can we simply establish that it's him, Alberto? I really have to get home." SinJin was shocked at himself, realizing that even though he knew Tam was all right, she still meant more to him than Pacal.

"Of course, I understand. Show me the way."

"Orlando didn't show you the tomb?"

"No, he was insistent upon waiting for you. Quite a loyal crew chief you have there."

"Well, it's right behind you." SinJin walked to the entrance and indicated a pile of rubble. "That's what we removed of the outermost wall. I think it's probably one of three, based on similarly dated tombs from other sites. Agreed?" Ramirez nodded. "If you look there," he pointed to a recess, "you'll see that we removed most of the second wall—enough to clear space for the final entrance. I waited for you to break through that last seal. By the book, Director." He smiled weakly, wanting desperately to get the approval to proceed and get home.

"Looks promising. Now, show me the glyphs that convinced you it's Shield Jaguar."

SinJin pointed to five rounded symbols on the inner wall. "For some reason, some of the glyphs are…"

"Backwards in order, I know." Ramirez examined the glyphs and began reading aloud.

"Also, I have a cacao cup that indicates ownership by Spear Jaguar and mentions his father. There are other pieces as well. I couldn't read them all, but Tamara could." Something pulled and poked at SinJin's brain, and he couldn't quite focus. What was it Tam had said? The glyphs on the pyramid were backwards in chronology, but only on the one side, and on this tomb slab. Everywhere else, they followed the standard Mayan chronology of rulers.

"Where did you see the backwards glyphs, Alberto?"

"Oh, everywhere, all over the site. Very unusual, not unheard of, though." He waved his hand to indicate the whole site.

A breeze blew around him, and dirt swirled near Ramirez's feet as he continued to study the glyphs. SinJin felt a tremor course through him.

"Listen, storyteller! Listen for the truth. Your beloved's life depends upon it!"

"Right." SinJin tried to sound nonchalant. His heart pounded fiercely in his ears. He could barely hear the noises of the birds and incessant buzzing of the insects. SinJin backed away from Ramirez.

"She is in danger!"

"I think you have it here, my friend. Well, *I* have it." He laughed in a way SinJin hadn't heard before. SinJin knew that Ramirez meant to own Pacal, at any cost. What had happened to obsess his friend? Why did he need this site so badly?

Ramirez backed out of the opening and brushed the dust off his pants. He reached to his hip, under his shirt.

"Don't."

He spun around and looked into the barrel of SinJin's revolver. "Well, well, well. Seems I underestimated the boy wonder. Always beating me to the punch, Twaine."

"Where is she?" SinJin's eyes were pure fire. "I'll kill you Alberto, I swear I will."

"No you won't. How will you find out where she is if you kill me?"

"If you hurt her in any way, I will kill you." SinJin swallowed back his fear, praying she wasn't dead already. His own life depended upon it.

"She's fine. Probably a little thirsty, a little frightened. She told quite a nice tale about your adventures together, your little dark escapades in the bedroom." SinJin hit him across the face with the butt of the gun and he crumpled to the ground.

Then SinJin heard the moan from the edge of the jungle. *Tam?* He turned for a second, in time to see Orlando staggering towards him. Time enough for Ramirez to pull out his gun and fire. SinJin fell, but before he passed out from the pain, he heard another shot ring out. Struggling to focus, he saw Rosa's son, José drop a gun, arm shaking. The boy had killed Alberto Ramirez.

Orlando staggered to the boy and held him close.

"Uncle! Are you all right?" José was crying and shaking.

"I think so. What made you come back, José, and with a gun!" Orlando struggled to get the words out, pain sweeping across his rugged face.

"Shield Jaguar told me to." Orlando looked at the boy in amazement, and then realized he must be in shock. He nodded towards SinJin. José knelt down and pressed on the wound to stop the bleeding. Orlando's strength gave out, and he sat on the ground next to SinJin and whispered orders to the boy. "I will stay with him. Get his keys, take the Land Rover."

"I don't really know how to drive."

"You do now, boy. Go."

Orlando watched the blood drain from Ramirez's chest onto the soil. He released SinJin for a moment to tie his shirt tightly around his own shoulder wound. It seemed that blood bathed all of Pacal. Even the first glimmers of the sunset were fiery red.

C· C· C·

Tam heard three shots. The first had jarred her awake. Many minutes later, two came close together. She prayed that it was hunters. At least they didn't hunt jaguars anymore, she thought. They were nearly extinct in these parts. She'd never live to see one. She fell back asleep.

C· C· C·

"My Husband, will it really happen that way? The evil man will die at the foot of your tomb?"

"Yes, love, it really will. Now close your eyes. I'll tell you the rest tomorrow."

Her eyes pleaded with him and she kissed his cheek. "Please?"

"Oh, all right, but come closer and rub my back."

"As you wish. Lord?"

"Hmnn?"

"I love you."

Shield Jaguar's heart shattered into a hundred pieces, and he pulled her close, pressed his lips on her head. "Ah, I had hoped as much."

Chapter Eleven

Jack did his best to reassure the Martins. They seemed too naïve, too sheltered, perhaps simply in shock, to really understand what was happening. They were an odd, intellectual couple, Jack thought, but they were kind. They looked baffled, as if they couldn't comprehend that anything bad could happen to anyone in the middle of research. He knew that they hadn't yet imagined the worst. He had.

As the plane touched down in Cancun, Jack prayed for the hundredth time that they would find Tam happily settled in at Cozmano, and that the worst the Martins would have to deal with was an eccentric new boyfriend. He was terrified that it wouldn't be that simple. Rosa wasn't a hysterical type, and it wasn't like Tam to take off and not tell anyone, especially her parents.

Jack looked at the handsome couple, wondering what they would think of Twaine. Well, he was certainly the least of their worries. Jack desperately sought for some way to help soften this blow for the Martins. Tam was the spitting image of Sandra, whose looks were holding up really well, Jack thought. Maybe a little more makeup, a better wardrobe—but the woman was an astrophysicist, after all. George didn't speak much, but he was clearly distraught.

They found their bags, grabbed a cab, and began the hour and a half drive to Twaine's house. It was already well past two in the morning. Hopefully she'd be there.

☾ ☾ ☾

SinJin woke and cursed. The burning in his shoulder was indescribable, but he felt the sting of a needle and knew he'd be numb soon enough. He tried to tell the nurse he didn't want the drug, but he couldn't shape the words and fell back into a troubled half-sleep.

Rosa sat near his hospital bed, holding his hand. "My baby, please help him." The tears rolled down her broad cheeks.

A young doctor strolled in and picked up SinJin's chart. He had heard Rosa's comment and lifted a brow. "You are his mother?" he asked in Spanish.

"Oh, no, his housekeeper. Please, doctor, will he survive?" The doctor tried not to laugh.

"Oh, Mama, please, relax. The bullet is out, and he lost a bit of blood. There's no infection at this point, he should be home with you tomorrow afternoon. Strong as an ox—good heart, good lungs. He's very lucky, all things considered. I'll give you prescriptions for antibiotics and painkillers to take with you."

The doctor patted the woman's hand and thought of the mess that had been brought in from the site of Pacal. The Mexican archaeologist, Ramirez, was dead. There had been very little blood left in his body. Orlando Rinaldo was luckier, but not as lucky as Professor Twaine. Rinaldo would need additional surgery to repair damage to his shoulder and collarbone. He had lost a lot of blood, but would no doubt recover fully.

The story had been incredible, and the doctor thought that the inquest might be rather interesting, hoping he might have to get involved. Evidently, this Ramirez had been quite a character. If he weren't dead, he'd face a variety of charges in Mexico City, including embezzlement as well as rumors about a rather young male student. It was ugly. The last pieces of the puzzle weren't together yet, though. The police were beginning to take the case of the missing Martin woman more seriously now. They hadn't launched a search, but would probably do so in the morning. He sighed. Hopefully she was off with another man. The alternative was unthinkable.

He reassured the matron again and left her to keep her unnecessary vigil at the Professor's bedside.

C C C

SinJin woke a few hours later and saw Rosa asleep in a nearby chair. He was foggy and tried to sip some water to clear the horrible taste from his mouth.

"Rosa," he hissed quietly. The woman stirred and looked at him. "Oh!" She hugged him, a little too tightly, and he winced in pain.

"Have they found her?"

"No, SinJin. They won't even look until morning."

"Fucking assholes. Get this off me." He indicated the IV needle and Rosa looked at him in horror.

"The bag's empty, Rosa, it's okay. I'm full of blood now." He saw he'd have to remove the needle himself. He was in agony. Whatever painkiller they had given him was wearing off, or hadn't been strong enough. Then he remembered vomiting from the drug. No wonder his mouth was so foul.

"Where's my wallet, my keys?" She glanced at the table near him and shook her head violently.

"Is the Land Rover here?"

"Si, Orlando's brother brought you both in it."

"Is Orlando alive?"

"He will live, but he must have surgery." She saw the pained look in his eyes. "No, no, the bone here," she pointed to her collarbone. "The doctor says he will be quite well." SinJin sighed.

"Ramirez?" His eyes burned.

"The son of a bitch is dead." SinJin lifted a brow in surprise. He had never known Rosa to curse.

"I think José shot him, but I can't quite trust my memory. That's when I passed out." SinJin shook his head, not able to take it in. Well, he would hear about José later, God bless the boy.

"No, no, please SinJin, you need rest." She was crying and he sat up, head spinning. He took her hand and kissed it.

"Mamacita, listen to me. Look into my eyes. I am fine. A little groggy, that's all. I know I must look bad, but you have to trust me. I would not lie to you. I will be fine. Okay?"

"No, no, no, not okay." She continued crying.

"Rosa, I can do this with you, or without you. It's your choice. I need you to drive." Her eyes widened at the prospect and she shook her head vehemently. "Well, it's time you learned now, isn't it? I should have taught you a long time ago. You are a modern woman, Rosa, we both know that." He did his best to smile. Even smiling hurt. Son of a bitch Ramirez.

The duty nurse ran after them as they passed her station, but SinJin held up his hand.

"You are part of a criminal case, Senor Twaine. I will notify the police if you leave!" The nurse picked up the phone and brandished it at SinJin.

"The Playa del Carmen police don't seem to give a damn about a woman in danger. See if they care about me."

SinJin began questioning his decision to have Rosa drive as they weaved and lurched down the highway, but after a half-hour or so, she seemed to have gotten the hang of it. He encouraged her, but took over when it was time to navigate the bumpy side road to Cozmano. As they drew up to the house, they saw someone on the porch. It was Jack Peders.

"What the hell?" SinJin ran his hand through his hair and groaned, the gesture sending waves of pain through his shoulder and arm.

"Any news?" Peders offered his hand. SinJin took it and shook his head. "Son of a bitch, what happened to you? You look like death."

The young man hugged Rosa. "It's good to see you, Rosa. I wish it were under better circumstances."

"Yes, Jack. Thank you for coming."

"Yes, thanks for coming, Peders. You never got word from her?"

"No." SinJin headed into the house and Jack ran in front of him to block his path.

"Professor Twaine. You have company."

"Obviously."

"No, more company. Tam's parents, the Martins. They're asleep in one of the bedrooms."

"What the hell did you bring them here for?"

"They have a right, Twaine. They're her *parents.*"

SinJin sighed and nodded. Jack was right, of course. He wasn't up to meeting his future in-laws. Or perhaps they'd never be his in-laws? He squeezed the thought down.

"What did happen? You were shot?" Jack indicated the bandage.

"It's fine. Alberto Ramirez is dead. Before he died, he shot our crew chief, Orlando."

Jack looked stunned. "The head of the service? How did he die? What's going on?"

"He's the one who took her, Jack. One of my boys shot him, or I'd be a dead man. It's complicated, and I'm not sure I understand it all, but I'll tell you and the Martins what I know."

"And he didn't tell you where she is? Before he died?" SinJin shook his head and saw Jack pale.

"God, she could be anywhere."

"Professor Twaine?" SinJin turned to find a man of about sixty years in his doorway. Professor George Martin, the most famous astrophysicist of his generation.

"Yes, Sir." He shook the man's hand. "I'm going to find your daughter."

"Yes, we will. What the hell happened to you? You're very pale. Come in here, boy." Canterbury, Tam had said. Of course, her parents were British. SinJin felt a bit dizzy and thought the man was right—it *was* time to sit down for a few minutes. He wouldn't do Tam any good if he was unconscious.

Rosa brewed coffee and joined the group in the living room. SinJin told Jack and the Martins what he knew, and Rosa filled in more details. Sandra Martin cried as her husband comforted her.

"So, SinJin, may I call you that?" Tam's pretty mother reached to take his hand.

"Of course, Dr. Martin."

"Call me Sandra. My daughter isn't only your assistant, is she?"

"No, Sandra."

"I didn't think so. You would be exactly her type. Brilliant, extraordinarily good looking, a little obsessive about your research." She tried to smile through the tears.

C C C

Tam looked at the stars through the window of the hut and fantasized about being with SinJin, sitting on the serene porch of Cozmano, sipping wine after one of Rosa's fantastic meals, talking about their fabulous discoveries. They would whisper through the night, and kiss, then SinJin would take her to bed, and make all her pain go away.

"Don't worry, storyteller, I am with you."

The voice was getting annoying now. All through the night, she had heard it, each time she had woken from her troubled naps. Tam knew that she was hallucinating. It was thirst, hunger, and fear. Tam had always thought she was tough, but one day without food and water had felt like a month. Her stomach clenched furiously. Her clothes were soaked with sweat and covered in dust. The air in the hut was stifling even in the cooler night. When the sun hit its zenith later in the day, she knew it would become unbearable. Tam had managed to remove the duct tape from her mouth by rubbing it against the pole. Screaming had done nothing but make her voice hoarse.

At least the phantom voice was encouraging and the horrible dreams of Shield Jaguar had stopped. She wondered idly how long it took to die of thirst. Her parents would know, she thought. And Jack, that's the sort of thing Jack would know. But Ramirez would kill her before she died of thirst.

Tam heard a rustling outside the hut. Ramirez! He had come for her. The tears flowed again and she struggled uselessly to free herself from her bonds. Then she saw it—a paw, scratching at the earth under the door.

A huge paw, as big as her hand. God help her! A wild creature would maul her before Ramirez got his chance. She saw a dark nose and watched it sniff the air.

She screamed as it jumped onto the high open window ledge. A jaguar! Its eyes burned into her and she saw the fury of the night predator. Her last thought before fainting was that she had finally managed to see a jaguar.

Tam came to and screamed again. The jaguar lay a few feet away, licking its paw, rubbing its ear. It was exquisite. Powerful muscles were apparent under his gorgeous coat. He turned to her suddenly and stood. The jaguar growled fiercely and Tam squeezed her eyes shut and prayed. Then she felt the pull at her bonds. The cat gnawed at the ropes, soaking her hands and wrists with his huge tongue. Tam shook in disbelief and fear.

"I'm losing my mind. Have you been speaking to me? Are you..."

The cat tilted his head and growled softly.

"Shield Jaguar?"

He growled again, more loudly, and Tam could have sworn the cat sounded annoyed with her for asking. She felt the ropes fall and rubbed her raw wrists, bringing painful life back to her hands as she looked at the jaguar. He pushed at her ankles with his nose and she began the difficult process of extracting her legs from the rope. The jaguar pushed her hands aside and pulled at the knot with his strong incisors, never scraping her skin. She was finally free, and fell to the ground. Tam cried as she stretched her aching legs. She looked at the cat, who seemed to be waiting for her.

"I don't know where I am, Shield Jaguar."

He growled again and hopped onto the window ledge. Of course, the jaguar certainly couldn't open the door's padlock. She'd have to get through the window. She pushed a huge empty barrel against the wall, every muscle in her body screaming in pain at the movements. Tam scrambled up and forced her body through the narrow opening. The drop wasn't very far, but she decided to start over and go through legs first so she could land on her feet. When she landed, the jaguar was again laying on the ground, grooming.

Well, Tam thought, I may be hallucinating, but it's better than sitting in that damned hut.

The cat stood and moved into the jungle, taking one of three paths spreading out from the hut's entrance.

"Hurry, he's waiting."

Tam followed on shaking legs. It was all she could do to keep up with the jaguar, even though his pace was slow.

Chapter Twelve

SinJin woke in a sweat. Damn, he hadn't meant to sleep, but had lain down for a moment to gain some strength, let his head clear. Two hours, and nearly light. He washed his face and hair and wiped down his body, wishing he could take a shower, but knowing the shoulder wouldn't take it.

Jack and George were on the porch, drinking coffee with Rosa.

"You look a bit better." George poured him coffee and pulled a pill out of his pocket.

"What is it? Painkillers make me sick."

"Not this one." He winked.

"Thanks. Listen, I think Ramirez was completely alone in this, but on the off chance someone else is out there, you should probably stay behind." SinJin knew what the answer would be, but had to try.

"Not a chance." George stood, draining his cup.

"Are you armed?" SinJin presented his revolver.

"Take the pill, I'll drive. Where are we going?"

"To the site. I don't know where else to start looking."

"Twaine, do you have another gun?" Jack surprised SinJin.

"Do you know how to use one, Jack? It's no game."

"I evidently shoot better than you. You missed me last year."

George looked taken aback. "You shot at our boy Peders here, Twaine?"

Jack waved him off. "It's an inside joke."

SinJin reached into the glove box of the Land Rover, handing Jack a small handgun. He was surprised when Jack comfortably checked the clip.

They were at the site at sunrise.

"This place still creeps me out," Jack said. "Oh, wow, you cleared this side. Look, One Smoke Rabbit, Two Smoke Monkey. Spear Jaguar? Hey, they're backwards!"

"How well do you read Mayan, Jack? I can't do that."

"You never gave me a chance."

"Asshole."

"What?"

"You mean, you never gave me a chance, *Asshole*. I can hear it in your voice. You may as well say it. Tam calls me that all the time. At least she did."

Jack flushed a little and SinJin wondered if he had been premature with Dr. Peders. There was something about the slender handsome dark-haired man that reminded him a little of Ramirez. Perhaps Jack's sexual preference *had* put him off, he thought regretfully. That *would* make him an asshole.

"Jack, I'm sorry. I'm sorry for last year. I really didn't know it was you, and I thought with someone plundering the site, perhaps he had made his way to the house... I don't generally shoot my assistants."

"Glad to hear it," George mumbled.

"And you hated that I'm gay."

SinJin took a deep breath. "And I suppose I hated that you're gay. I'll try to explain sometime."

"No need. I think I may understand better than you think. Apology accepted. But Twaine?"

"What?"

"You owe me another apology. I'm a good archaeologist."

"So Tam says." SinJin pulled at his hair, looking around the site, at the fringe of jungle that seemed endless.

"Fuck you, Ramirez!" He sat on the step of the pyramid, looking helplessly at his companions. "I don't know where to start. There's nothing in any direction for at least two miles. She could be anywhere."

George sat next to SinJin. "Twaine, listen, be logical. He certainly didn't carry her very far, and not from Cozmano, correct? So, if he was in a vehicle, there's no reason to suspect that she is near the site?"

"No, she's close. He didn't have the time to take her very far and be here at the site when I met him. His car was here. Anyway, I know she's close."

George looked at Jack, who shrugged. A lover's intuition wasn't much to go on.

"Are there any other roads leading away from the site?"

"Quiet!" They all heard it, a rustle in the underbrush. SinJin motioned with his gun for the men to join him behind a pile of tumbled building stones.

"Oh my God!" Jack whispered, unable to believe his eyes. A large cat strolled from the jungle, and stopped suddenly, focused in their direction.

"Don't shoot it, Jack, it's a jaguar." Impossible, SinJin thought.

Favoring one leg, the beast made its way up the pyramid, winding side to side amongst the vines and branches. Perched on the top, he looked down at the men, who stood now in clear view to get a better look. And in an instant, he was gone.

"Tell my story, SinJin!"

A chill ran down SinJin's spine and he felt Jack grip his arm in desperate fear.

"Bloody hell." George looked as if he would faint.

Well, SinJin thought, for once, everyone had heard the voice. But what did it matter? She was gone.

"Help me find her, Shield Jaguar! Damn it, help me find her!" He dropped his face into his hands and looked as if he would weep.

"I'm here, Professor." The three turned. Tam clung to a tree trunk. She was bloody, filthy, and scratched, her face badly bruised. "And I think I'd really like to go home now."

And unlike the first time she passed out in front of him, SinJin reached Tam in time to catch her.

☾ ☾ ☾

Dr. Martinez breathed out deeply, sounding relieved.

"Move aside, Professor Twaine, or I cannot examine her. In fact, you should join the others in the waiting room." He glanced at SinJin as he took Tam's pulse and listened to her heart, thinking that it would take an army to pull this man away.

"Professor, let me begin by saying that if you are going to take care of this girl, and I assume from the look on your face that you intend to do so, you will have to take better care of yourself. I'm in charge here. Now sit down and shut up!" SinJin sat, startled by the man's manner.

"She is a little dehydrated," he motioned for the nurse to set up an IV for fluids. "She is a little abraded here and here." He wiped away some blood. "She has been hit by an object here, but nothing seems to be broken." He snapped out an order for the nurse to arrange for an X-ray of Tam's cheek. "Her heart rate is normal, and her blood pressure is slightly low, probably because of the dehydration. That should change rapidly."

"That's it?"

"Yes, that seems to be it. She's exhausted, and is sleeping. I have given her something to ensure that she stays asleep for a while longer. I see people in worse shape from Spring Break parties. Actually, Professor, you are in far worse shape than she is. I would strongly suggest that you allow me to readmit you to this hospital and continue the treatment that you so recklessly abandoned. Am I clear? Look man, you're deathly pale and in shock. Now that she's safe, your body is starting to shut down. I'm not exaggerating your condition. The surgeon who removed that bullet would be stunned to know what you did last night. Why not get better for her as quickly as possible?"

"Can I have that bed?" SinJin indicated one a few yards from Tam.

The doctor laughed. "I somehow expected you would ask that. This isn't a resort, now, keep that in mind. But room service is open twenty-four hours a day."

SinJin managed a weak laugh. "Thanks, doctor."

"You are very welcome. Congratulations on finding her."

"Oh, someone else found her." He lay on the bed and stared at Tam as the nurse worked on cleaning her up.

C C C

SinJin woke to the site of Tam, leaning on one arm, staring at him.

"Hey handsome." Her voice was weak and he knew she was trying to sound lighthearted for his sake.

"Tam." His heart was going to burst, he was sure of it. He sat up quickly and took her in. SinJin felt silly, uncertain what she would want him to do. He had been in such pain, thinking she had left him. It had lingered and left a trail of doubt.

"Doctor says we're both going to live. Imagine that."

"Yes, imagine that." He smiled and the dam burst. She began sobbing.

"Tam, that note, it was Ramirez, right?"

"You know what, Professor Twaine? I have it so bad for you that I think they might have to keep me in here and treat me for it."

SinJin's heart welled over. For the second time in less than a day, he pulled out his IV. He went to her and knelt by her bedside. She was a few inches from him. He looked into her eyes and let her gaze wash over him. She put a tentative hand on his cheek and he moved closer and kissed her delicately. Then he buried his face in her embrace.

"Oh, Tam. I thought you dumped me. Then I thought you were dead. I died myself, you can't understand. I'm so sorry you got caught up in this, it's my fault. That crazy son of a bitch!"

"I'm fine, Sinj. It's all right now." He sat on the side of her bed and held her tightly, not feeling the pain in his shoulder, not feeling anything but her warmth. He stretched out and held her against his chest.

"Sinj? Um, we're still, like, a couple, right?"

He smiled and nodded. "Yes, idiot."

She sighed and smiled. "I have to tell you something, and I know you're going to think I'm crazy."

"No, I won't, trust me."

"Yes, I think you will. Ramirez had me tied to a pole in a hut, not far from the site."

"He didn't hurt you in any way? Please, Tam, tell me."

"No. Not like that. He hit me on the cheek, but no, he didn't touch me."

"I couldn't break free of the ropes." She showed him her wrists, which were covered in bandages. "I tried."

"How did you get them off?"

"An animal chewed through them. I know it sounds preposterous."

"The cat led you to the site." He looked into her eyes.

"You saw it?"

"Yes, we all did."

"All?"

"Jack, George, and I. We heard it speak too, all three of us."

"Jack and my father are here? My mother? Oh my God. They must have been terrified. Wait a minute. They *heard* it?"

"Never mind, I'll tell you about it later. Just rest now."

"Sinj, I don't want to rest. I want to leave. I want to go home."

"What do you mean by 'home'?"

"Cozmano. What else would I mean?"

He kissed her again and then pulled her close and whispered into her ear. "Dr. Martin? Don't leave me again. That's an order."

The doctor walked in and laughed loudly at the pair, locked in a deep kiss. "I'd say 'get a room,' but it seems you've already done that."

Chapter Thirteen

Jack thought SinJin looked a little lost amidst Tam's reunion with her parents. He tentatively took a seat next to him on the porch. He thought the man looked healthier, happier, but still anxious for some reason.

"Quite a week, Professor."

No answer. Jack stood. The guy was still a jerk.

"Sit down, Jack." Annoyed, Jack sat, wondering why this man was so powerful that one felt the need to do what he said.

They sat in silence, sipping coffee, listening to the jungle sounds, and the occasional burst of laughter coming from the living room.

"She seems well enough, SinJin. You seem better too."

"I'm fine."

"You don't seem *fine,* just a bit better. Man, you rescued the girl, the bad guy is dead, what's the problem?"

"Well, we both know I didn't rescue the girl, don't we?"

"I don't think I'll ever be ready to talk about that one. I don't get it, and I don't want to get it." He couldn't help probing a little, though. "We all heard the same voice, right? 'Tell my story.'"

172

"I'm not sure I'll get the chance to tell his story. Who knows what will happen to Pacal now?"

"Oh damn, I'm sorry, I can't believe I didn't tell you. The guy from the archaeological service called to check on your condition. He's a temporary replacement for Ramirez. They've evidently flipped out over what happened. He's coming to see you tomorrow."

"What?"

"I'm really sorry, I zoned. With Tam and all."

"That's okay." SinJin was gruff. "Did he say anything about the site, about me? I mean, did he give any indication of what they intend to do?"

"Oh, sure. He's bringing the permit for you and some papers to sign for your appointment to the University faculty."

"Are you sure?" He held Jack by the shoulders and examined his expression.

"Quite sure. Oh, you thought you'd lose the site? No, they're very hot on you continuing the work. Even talked about finding funding for it."

Jack smiled and SinJin slowly returned his smile and then closed his eyes. Jack could practically feel the tension drain away from the man.

"Geez, I'm really sorry. I thought you'd assume that part would work out."

SinJin was pinching the bridge of his nose and looked pained.

"Jack, I hope you'll stay on," he nearly whispered.

"What?"

"Stay on at the site. Work. You know, archaeology?"

"Why?"

"Well, because you're a good archaeologist, at least that's what you say, and I'm going to need a lot of help with this tomb. If it's what I think it is, I mean, what I know it is." He laughed nervously. "I haven't quite gotten used to knowing that it really is his tomb."

"Oh, it's him all right."

"Then I'll need someone to manage the objects we recover, the storeroom, and restoration. I'll need you to set it up while I'm at the site. We'll hire some more help, but I want to keep all the crew I have now. Orlando stays in charge of the men. He's certainly earned that right. And well, let's see, we'll get you settled in somewhere. There's a little group of houses nearby for sale. Fifty-percent more than last year's wage."

"Offer accepted." Jack's heart was racing. It was beyond anything he had hoped for.

"Good. And Jack, I'm sorry, again."

"I guess it's none of my business, but I think I understand. The business about Ramirez and the young student. I know you can handle yourself, but did he hit on you?"

"Endlessly. But it's weird, because otherwise, we were friends. We felt the same way about the work." SinJin shook his head. "I still can't understand why he lost it like that."

"Put it aside, SinJin. For Tam's sake, if not your own."

SinJin nodded.

"Besides, Professor, you aren't my type, so don't worry about me." Jack stood, trying to break the dark mood.

"Why the hell not? I thought I was everyone's type!" Jack groaned. "Let's go in."

SinJin thought his house had never seemed more alive, more interesting. Rosa fussed over Tam and the Martins. He watched Tam as she brought her mother up to speed on the week's events. He heard a mention of Vista del Mar, strawberries, roses, and chocolates. She couldn't be talking about their night of sex to her mother! His eyes grew huge as he listened more closely. Yes, she was filling Sandra in on the details of their time together.

"Um, Tam, can I interrupt for a minute? I suppose you all know that they're giving me, well us, the site. I'll get the permit tomorrow." Tam smiled broadly, proudly.

"And the appointment still stands. So, I'll be staying on here for quite a while, I suppose. Jack has taken the job of artifact supervisor, and I'll need to hire more crew. Well, anyway, we can work that all out later. I have to be at the site tomorrow with the new guy. What's his name?" He looked at Jack.

"Pulido."

"And I guess I'll be pretty busy for a while. But, um, George and Sandra, I hope you'll stay on for a while. You can stay here, or at Vista del Mar."

"Oh, I don't think our family finances can quite handle Vista del Mar, Sinj." Tam laughed.

"What? Oh, that's not a problem, Tam."

"We're not charity cases, honey," George quickly defended himself.

"No, that's not what I meant." He looked at Tam and felt a flush of embarrassment. "Sorry, I should have told you. I own Vista del Mar. When I said I was paying a lot for the room, I was lying. For effect." He began blushing. Tam smiled. "Well, the suite does usually go for a lot! Anyway, I was hoping you'd stay around for a bit, visit with Tam, be my guests. It's been a rough few days. She could use your company."

Sandra looked at George and nodded. "That would be lovely, Professor."

"Now, Tam, could we have a minute?" He pulled her by the hand and led her off the porch and into the fringe of the jungle.

"Where are we going?"

"Nowhere. Here will do." He looked into her eyes and felt the heat build in his heart, in his body. He had Pacal, he had Shield Jaguar. Now he needed her. He brushed a strand of pale hair away from her bruised cheek. He crushed her lips with his.

"I thought about this moment, over and over again. About holding you, kissing you."

"I'm in love with you, SinJin Twaine. Is that what you need to hear?"

"Yes! I need to hear it as many times as you can stand to say it."

He was hard and pressed against her stomach.

She moaned and pushed her hand into his loose shorts. "My God, I'll never get enough of this." She rubbed her hand up and down the length of him.

"Not here, not like this," he panted.

"Yes, here, right now, like this." She pulled up her sundress and he ripped off her thong, leaving her bare. He pushed her against a tree, eyes on fire. He turned her around to face the tree and thrust his swollen cock into her quickly. She cried out and he whispered, "Hold on to that tree, baby." He felt the heat inside her as he thrust forcefully, as she clenched onto his cock. They cried aloud as they came together. SinJin kept her pinned against the tree and gently kissed her neck and shoulder.

"Sorry that was so quick, Dr. Martin." He was panting and sweating, and not simply from the passion. "No, don't turn around yet." He held her hands against the tree with one hand as he reached into his pocket. "Now look at the ground, no peeking." He slipped the ring onto her left ring finger and she gasped. "Okay, you can look."

"Oh my God." He had bought her a ring. When had he done that? She couldn't see it very clearly through her tears and he helped her wipe them away. Then she took it in. "Oh my God! SinJin! No!" She couldn't take her eyes off the stone.

"No?"

"It's exquisite. I've never seen anything so beautiful. But isn't it worth the gross national product of a small nation? I mean, *honestly.*"

He laughed and hugged her. "Oh Tam, you make me so happy. Are you happy? Please tell me you're happy. I don't have anything else to offer. It's me, this house, and Pacal. Those are my life. And you. Is that going to be enough to keep you? You won't get tired of it here?"

"SinJin, you can't mean this. Are you sure it's not the kidnapping—I mean, maybe you're still shaken? You don't need to do this to keep me here, I won't want to leave like Laura did. I promise."

"Can we do this soon? I mean, really soon."

She mouthed a silent "Oh."

☾ ☾ ☾

Jack looked at the Martins, who were a little red in the face. Rosa was laughing. They had heard the couples' cries of passion clearly.

"I guess they missed each other," Jack shrugged.

The Martins couldn't help laughing at that.

"I think they got engaged." They looked at Rosa in surprise.

"Wouldn't that be a little soon?" Sandra looked very confused.

"Well, he bought a ring for her. I was with him. A pink diamond. Very rare." She imitated the shopkeeper.

Sandra smiled at her husband. "Well, dear, your proposal was a little more sedate than that, wasn't it? I feel a little cheated, actually."

"Yes, I feel rather embarrassed now. Sorry dear. Wish I could do the moment over."

Chapter Fourteen

Estuardo Pulido was a short, stocky man of middle years. He seemed terribly nervous, and SinJin had to reassure the archaeologist repeatedly that he held Ramirez alone responsible for the horrible events at Pacal.

"Your permit, sir. Begin excavating the tomb and the buildings associated with Pacal when you like. Please submit the catalog of artifacts quarterly. For the time being, they can come to me. And the paperwork for your appointment." He searched SinJin's face, evidently fearing he would reject the Professorship and take his expertise elsewhere. Without Twaine, the site was vulnerable to looters. Pulido didn't have the resources to handle it now. SinJin signed the papers without a word and handed them back to the man.

Pulido sighed, relieved. "And we will begin the process of securing funding for the excavation immediately. Now, Señor, if it not too much trouble, I would dearly love to see the tomb."

"It would be my great pleasure."

SinJin, Tam, and Jack were happy to have the crew back and answered their many questions while they gave Pulido a short tour.

"Where's José?" Tam asked.

"Here, Dr. Martin."

She gave the young man a hug, and kissed his cheek. "Thank you for giving me my SinJin, José." Tears filled her eyes.

"I am not the one to thank, miss. I just did what he told me to do."

"Who's that, boy?" Pulido asked.

SinJin glanced sharply at Tam and she put her finger to her mouth to silence José, who cast his boss a sly glance.

"It's a long story, Dr. Pulido. Let me tell you some other time. Now, let me show you the tomb."

The entire crew followed the archaeologists to the tomb entrance. Tam and Jack were on their bellies immediately, discussing the symbols.

"Kids, back away so our visitor can see for himself."

Pulido squatted and ran his hand over the glyphs, a gesture it seemed no one could resist. "Amazing," he stood. "I'm not as good as the 'kids,' here, Professor, but it's fairly clear what you have."

SinJin described the sequence of walls and pointed to the innermost seal, as he had described to Ramirez.

Pulido smiled. "Señor, as they say in your country, 'go for it.'"

Feeling as if he were moving in a dream, SinJin took the pick-axe that Jack handed to him and chipped away at an undecorated stucco wall. There was room for him alone in the narrow passage, and it took two hours for him to widen a space big enough to fit through. Tam and Jack stayed by his side the entire time, taking notes, measurements, and photos to record the work. The wall was carefully removed, one tiny chunk at a time, so it wouldn't fall into the chamber.

"Your shoulder? Do you want a break?" Jack asked.

"I'm fine," he replied.

A short time later, he backed out of the space and stood, brushing himself off. "I'm too big." He looked crushed. "If I widen it anymore, so that it's big enough for me to get in there, I could damage the supporting beams. The tomb is below the opening." He looked at Tam and she grinned.

She squirmed into the hole and darkness swallowed her.

"Flashlight," she called back. And moments later, she backed out and looked at SinJin. "A stone sarcophagus. I've never seen anything like it. On the lid, it reads, something like, 'Shield Jaguar, Lord of Pacal, fearful enemy, revered by Spear Jaguar'." She shivered and thought of the animal that had led her to safety. The sun fell behind clouds and shade blanketed the site once again.

"And?" SinJin urged.

"It's intact. Never been touched." The crew cheered, talked excitedly and SinJin clapped his hands and joined in. Tam and Jack watched in amazement as he did a little dance with José.

"Some beast, eh Jack?"

"You tamed him, Tam. Amazing."

Pulido took his hand. "Congratulations, Professor. I will look forward very much to your report."

They worked as long as the light lasted, sketching a plan for supporting the structure as they removed the outer wall. They would remove the coffin from the side, rather than dismantle the high structure above it. Tomorrow, tomorrow they would see the bones of the ancient ruler.

☾ ☾ ☾

Dinner was a celebration, held on the porch of Cozmano, and Tam felt a peace that had been so elusive since she arrived in Mexico.

Jack broke the tranquility. "So, SinJin, tell us, which is better, getting the girl or getting the permit?" Tam scowled at him.

SinJin reached into his shirt pocket, pulled out the folded permit, and held it in front of Jack's face.

"If Tam asked me to rip this up right now, the day before opening Shield Jaguar's tomb, I would."

"Hell, no!" She snatched the paper from him, trying to lighten the mood. "I'd be out of a job. He didn't mean any harm, honey."

"I know," he rubbed his hand through his hair. "Sorry Jack. Damn, I'm always apologizing to you."

"No, that was stupid. I knew the answer anyway."

SinJin barely heard him. He looked at Tam. She felt his stare and smiled, but she knew something was terribly wrong. He looked so tense.

They held each other's eyes and Jack, Rosa, and the Martins knew it was time to leave them alone.

"Sit down, Tam." SinJin ran his hand through his hair.

"What is it, Sinj? It was an incredible day. You have to be thrilled."

"A fucking incredible day. But it wouldn't have meant shit if you hadn't been there with me. You, it's you. You don't feel the same way I do. It's killing me."

"I don't understand."

"Yes you do. You understand perfectly. You don't want to admit it. You don't want to hurt me after everything we've been through, after Ramirez."

"You're wrong."

"No, I'm not wrong. If you've changed your mind, you have to tell me, Tam. Don't make a fool of me."

There it was, the dark distant look he had when she first met him. He was shutting down, terrified. She leaned close to him and touched his cheek, caressed him. "Sinj, look at me. I'm not falling in love with you anymore."

She felt his muscles stiffen.

"I'm there. I'm completely, fully, absolutely in love with you. I would go through it all again to have the chance to sit like this with you, to look at your beautiful face, to touch you, to wear your ring. I can't remember a time when I didn't feel this way. You overwhelm me. You terrify me with your intensity. I'm obsessed with you sexually, even though I don't think I'll ever be enough for you. You are the weirdest guy I know. You are the most wonderful man I've ever met. I can't believe you want me."

"Oh my God." He buried his face in her chest. He was nearly shaking with relief. He looked up after a minute. "Then you will marry me?"

"Absolutely, Professor. I don't understand why you started doubting me."

"I don't know either. It seems impossible that I can have everything I want. Three days." He kissed her hand. "We'll go to the court in Cancun tomorrow after work, sign the papers—you do have your birth certificate, right. Then we can be married two days later."

"I can't be ready in three days! Are you kidding!" She laughed nervously. "You've been in the jungle too long."

He looked stunned. "What do you mean? Then you really don't want it?"

"No, that's not what I said. It's just too soon."

"Then you don't want it?"

"Sinj, give me a little time!"

"What's *time* going to do? Either you want me, or you don't. I'm not a kid, Tam. I'm not going to change. There's not much more to me than what you see. Oh hell, let me know when you're ready, then." He was in the Land Rover and gone before she could think of the right words.

Rosa found her on the porch, crying silently.

"Oh, baby, what now? You two, what's happening?"

"He wants me to marry him in three days. He's angry at me. I need more time."

"Three days!" Rosa clapped her hands and laughed, eyes twinkling mischievously. "That's my SinJin, doesn't fool around."

"It's not funny, Rosa. Do you realize how long I've known him? What kind of idiot gets married that quickly? Doomed to failure."

"Yes, I suppose my Ricky and I are the only couple who managed to stay together after such a courtship. No other couple in the world ever did it. You must be right. SinJin is insane. In any case, the man never seems to know what he really wants. Not a good decision maker."

"Very funny. That's not helpful."

"Tamara, I watched you flirt with him the second day you knew him. I know you were in his arms that very night. I watched you fall in love with him. I saw his face when he read that letter. It wasn't the face of a man who only cares for the bedroom. It's your choice. Do you want him? Forever?"

"Of course I want him."

"You aren't sure. Look, baby, SinJin is a little different. His family, well, they were a little different. His sister is too, trust me. He's not going to change. If you don't like him the way he is, don't marry him. Don't marry him for the site."

"I would never do that. I would die before hurting him."

"You almost did, Tamara. Let me ask you one more thing. When you were locked up in that hut, what did you think about?" She wiped her hands on her apron and returned to the kitchen, without waiting for Tam's answer.

Tam allowed herself to think carefully of her captivity for the first time since escaping. What had she thought about? Oh God.

She waited on the porch for two hours. He finally pulled up. He saw her and stood by the car, knowing it was important.

She stood and put her hands on her hips. "Three days. And that's the last favor I ever do for you, Professor." He grinned.

C C C

Tam woke in a panic.

"I don't have a dress, shoes, anything. We don't have rings. We can't, it's not possible."

"Tam. Stop." He grabbed her shoulders. "Do you remember the day we worked at the site, went to the beach, went shopping?"

"Sinj, that was a few days ago, of course I remember." She flushed, remembering every detail of the day, especially the night.

"Today we'll go to work as usual. We'll drive to Cancun and fill out some papers. We'll go shopping, then we'll come home. I've taken care of everything else. Understand?"

"What do you mean, you've taken care of everything else? How could anything be taken care of?"

"Trust me. The staff of Vista del Mar knows what they're doing. They better, I pay them enough. Especially the Resort Director."

He brought his mouth down on hers and made her forget her fears, at least for a moment. The heat rose and he brought his hand to her breast and began nibbling on her ear, whispering sinful fantasies.

"Hello?" Jack pulled them apart. "We're still here."

"Oh. Sorry."

They turned when they heard the Volkswagen. "Who is this?"

Rosa ran to the car and hugged the young brunette who climbed from it. She was on the short side and was about as stylish as a girl could get, with a great plump body stuffed into a perfect black dress and spiked heals. Her hair was short and bobbed back and forth, as she ran to the porch.

"Who is it, Sinj?" Tam wondered about the cute woman who evidently knew Rosa so intimately.

"It's your wedding planner." Tam looked at him and he hugged her and kissed her forehead. "Aw, you look jealous, baby. I like that." He whispered, "As a matter of fact, I might have to find a way to make you jealous more often."

"Do that and you'll die."

The woman ran up the stairs and was scooped up into SinJin's arms and spun around.

"Hi handsome."

"Hi baby." He kissed her cheek and Tam felt herself flaring up.

"Oh, and you are the famous Tamara Martin! Oh, you're beautiful, he wasn't kidding." She hugged Tam and kissed her on the cheek as if she had known her forever.

Then she lowered her voice and became very serious. "I'm very sorry to hear about what you went through. I'm glad you're all right. SinJin was sick over you."

Cynthia smiled suddenly. "Well, we have a lot of work to get done in a few days! I'm glad I got you before you went to the site—I want to go over some things."

"You really are a wedding planner?"

"It seems I am for the next few days. I'm good at parties, dinners, that sort of thing. And I run a resort. So your fiancé thought I might be able to help pull off this ridiculous stunt. Actually, you're going to be thrilled with my ideas, I'm sure of it. Wait until you see the menu. God! I'm fucking brilliant."

The Martins and Jack looked confused. "I'm sorry," SinJin shook his head. "Cynthia, these are Tam's parents and our friend, Jack Peders. This is my sister, Cynthia. She runs the Vista del Mar, where the wedding is going to be held."

Tam punched SinJin in the arm. "Trying to make me jealous over your sister. That's sick."

Cynthia waved her hand. "Okay, women inside, men on your own. Do whatever the hell is it you do at times like these, which is probably nothing." She grabbed Tam by the arm and pulled her into the living room.

SinJin called after them. "One hour, Cynthia my love, one hour. Then we have to go to work, understand?"

"Yes sir!" She saluted SinJin and Tam had to laugh.

Cynthia whispered in her ear. "He's such an ass. Don't you just love him, though? Oh, of course you do, you're marrying him." She giggled.

In one hour, nearly to the minute, Cynthia had nailed down flowers, food, decorations, vows, music, photos, the works. The woman was a whirlwind, and Tam's head spun.

"Great! That's about all I need today! Aw, sweetie, you look exhausted, I'm sorry. It's a lot, I know." She widened her dark brown eyes for a minute and examined Tam carefully. "You really love him?"

"Oh yes. I really do."

"Well, I'm biased. He's really good looking, don't you think? I've been trying to set him up for a few years now—he wouldn't have any of them. Said they were boring. I think I know what he meant, but it's not the kind of thing a sister discusses with her brother. He's not *deviant*, is he?" She giggled a little and wiggled her eyebrows.

"God, Cynthia, I can't discuss that." Tam's cheeks were on fire.

"There's my answer! I knew it!" She laughed. "Rosa, come here. Haven't you ever wondered about SinJin? I mean, what kind of *lover* he would make. He seems so dark, and mysterious. Ah, my Blake could use a good dose of dark and mysterious in the bedroom."

"Please, Cynthia, stop." Tam couldn't help laughing.

"Oooh, we'll have to have a girls' night out before the wedding. Of course, that would have to be tomorrow night, I suppose. That's it, we'll go into Playa tomorrow night. Pick you up at eight." She was gone before Tam could protest.

Tam wandered onto the porch in a daze.

"All done with the wedding plans?" SinJin asked.

"Did you two really have the same parents?"

He laughed. "I can't figure it out, either. But I guarantee one thing. You won't be disappointed. She runs Vista del Mar like a machine."

"Come here." Tam sat on SinJin's lap and they locked lips. Jack groaned.

"Oh, relax, Jack," George chided. "At least they aren't having sex twenty yards away from us this time."

Chapter Fifteen

In two hours, the crew had pulled away a bit more of the wall and replaced it with wooden beams to keep the roof secure. The sarcophagus was now fully visible. SinJin and Jack worked with painstaking care to slide the flat top off, inch by inch.

Layers of disintegrated cloth covered the body. Wound within the layers were dried flowers and tiny statues. Tam caught her breath each time SinJin removed a piece, photographed it, and put it into a numbered box. Closer and closer to the body, the wrappings revealed more impressive treasures; an exquisite flint knife, with the most incredibly complex carvings they had ever seen. Jade and coral beads, a gold pendant. Finally, with the entire crew holding their breath, praying that the skeleton was complete and intact, SinJin peeled away the last layer.

Exquisite, perfect, heartwrenching—a small skeleton, arms folded across his chest, the remnants of a headdress around his skull. Tam cried, and she knew SinJin wanted to. It wasn't spectacular, she thought. It wasn't covered in layers of gold or surrounded by incredible jewels. It was the bare skeleton of a man who had governed a city and ruled a people. It was simply a man, who had no doubt been proud, who had no doubt been a ruthless warrior, a terrifying enemy, who had children who buried him with reverence. Just a man.

Tam looked at SinJin, who was transfixed. He closed his eyes, and she thought he must have been praying for the long-dead king. Then she heard it, as clearly as the rest did.

"Tell my story."

SinJin put his arm around Tam and rested his head on her shoulder. He would spend many years uncovering the secrets that Pacal had yet to tell, and he would spend his career telling the King's story. And Tam would help him do it.

"Look," Jack pointed to one of the leg bones. "It's broken." A chill ran down Tam's spine. "Well, that would explain the jaguar's limp, I suppose." He laughed, but Tam knew he wasn't joking.

"All right, Jack, you're in charge." Tam couldn't believe her ears. SinJin was going to let someone else pack up the skeleton for shipment to the University. They had to do it perfectly and quickly, or the remains would deteriorate rapidly. Jack nodded, seemingly undaunted by the task, and SinJin patted him on the back. "You can do this, Jack. I won't even shoot you if you screw up."

He turned to Tam. "We have a little work ahead of us, don't we?"

"Years."

"No, I mean today. Jack will take care of our friend, here. Come on, everyone's waiting for us at home."

C C C

He wasn't kidding. It seemed that Cynthia had drafted everyone into wedding preparations. The Martins, SinJin, Cynthia, and Rosa descended upon Cancun with a vengeance. After securing the marriage license, they wandered the more exclusive shops like a pack of wolves. Tam, Rosa, and Sandra found dresses and shoes, and Rosa pulled Tam into a lingerie shop. George and SinJin grabbed tuxedos off the rack and did the best they could for Jack who was still at the site. They found simple platinum bands, and in four hours, had done everything needed.

They ate at a seaside restaurant and arrived at Cozmano exhausted. Jack finally returned from the site, looking sore, filthy, and exhilarated. He didn't wait for SinJin's questions. It was too important to be coy.

"Done. And beautifully, if I do say so myself. The men are guarding the site tonight—I figured that's what you'd want."

SinJin sighed in relief.

The Martins were already packed, and Jack gathered his things to check into Vista del Mar. SinJin drove them to the resort and saw them safely installed, and then returned home, dying for a chance to have time with Tam. To discuss the day, and lay with her, look at her, make love to her. He arrived at nearly the exact moment his sister did. They found Tam out cold, sleeping like a baby.

"So much for girls' night out," Cynthia sighed.

"So much for boy's night in," SinJin laughed.

SinJin worked through a good part of the evening, checking through Jack's notes and adding his own. He fell asleep in the storage hut, glasses still on. Rosa found him at midnight and pulled him to his bedroom. Five o'clock came very early.

C· C· C·

The bride was frantic. She hid it as well as she could, directing the workers while SinJin and Jack prepared the storage facility. What had she done? She didn't know this man at all! He was strange, aloof, a loner, obsessed with archaeology. He spoke to dead Mayan kings! So did she! She must be insane. When the men still hadn't returned, she took a lift to Cozmano with the workers.

"Pick up the pace, honey. It's time." Cynthia started collecting Tam's wedding things, and Rosa was packing her suitcase.

"What are you talking about?"

The women looked at her pathetically.

"You are getting married in less than twenty-four hours. Or did you forget? We missed girls' night out. We sure as hell aren't missing this day."

"But SinJin? I have to see him before tomorrow."

"Honey, that's not the idea. The idea is to see him tomorrow, not before. Besides, think what he's going to feel..." Cynthia giggled.

SinJin returned to a find her gone. George and Jack had to reassure him continually that this was normal female behavior. She hadn't gone away. It would all be fine. He went to bed in a tumult, worrying, wondering. She wouldn't change her mind, she wouldn't.

C C C

When Tam looked into the mirror, she thought for a moment she was dreaming. Her pale shimmering short dress, her hair neatly swept up with a flower tucked in the chignon, a bouquet in her hands. Who was this stranger?

Rosa pulled her along through the walkways of the resort to the little bridge that crossed over a stream. It was paradise. She stopped cold. There were at least two hundred people! Nearly all locals, dressed in their finest. Cynthia saw her and motioned her to pick up the pace. Her father was waiting for her.

"Are you all right, honey? You look a little shocked. You don't have to do this, you know."

Then she saw him. A god. A god in a tuxedo. Hair brushed away from his perfect face, eyes gleaming brightly in anticipation, a nervous grin. A tear slid down her face and she brushed it away.

"Oh my God, Dad. He's the most beautiful thing I've ever seen in my life. How did I get so lucky?" George smiled and took her arm.

"Let's go, baby. He's waiting for you."

SinJin took in a breath when he saw her. Gorgeous, elegant, sexy, perfect.

He coughed and Jack looked at him in concern. "Doing okay there, pal?"

"Just can't take it in, Jack. She showed up. She showed up."

"Course buddy. She's been waiting for you her whole life. Why wouldn't she show up?"

"Because stuff like this only happens in dreams."

☾ ☾ ☾

How could she be nervous? After what she had shared with this man already, how could she possibly worry about tonight? Tam thanked each guest as the reception drew to a close. There had been hours of food and drink and dancing like nothing Tam had ever seen. Cynthia had made it perfect, but the warm people of Cozmano had made it unforgettable. Tam had danced in SinJin's arms, smelled the delicious cologne wafting from his warm skin, kissed his incredible lips, and caressed his perfect face. He had told her she was exquisite, the love of his life.

"You're ready, Dr. Martin? Or is it Martin-Twaine?"

"Just Martin."

"I expected that."

"You're okay with that?"

"I'm okay with everything about you. Might even consider that co-author clause to our contract. By the way, I think you owe me a lap dance."

"The season isn't over."

"Come on, time to start."

"Start what, Professor?"

"A lifetime of mind-blowing sex with your husband, of course."

He led her to their bungalow at a fast clip, her heels clicking on the pathway as he pulled off his tie and jacket, unbuttoned his cuffs.

Sexy. God he was sexy. It couldn't be real. She looked down at her hand again. They were married. She looked at his hand. Yep, he wore one too.

She kicked off her shoes in an effort to keep up with him. He took them from her and threw them into the bushes.

"You know, husband, I'm beginning to think you're a little twisted. An animal. A sexual beast."

He lifted her into the air and threw her over his good shoulder in reply. They reached their door and he opened it without putting her down. She gasped when he threw her on the bed. The intoxicating scent of hundreds of roses filled the room. Candles burned on every available inch of table space. He pulled off his shirt, shoes and socks and knelt beside her on the bed. He handed her a box.

Tam opened it and gasped. Dozens of emeralds, hanging from strands of gold. "Oh my God."

"That's a good 'oh my God'?"

"Oh, Professor, I don't know what to say." She began to tear up. "You make me cry so much. Who would have thought the Beast would be such a softy?" He fastened the necklace on her.

Tam looked into his eyes and she saw the need building in him. She wasn't ready, she saw that he recognized her hesitancy.

"Let's have one glass of champagne," he suggested. "I didn't get a drop at the reception. I was too nervous."

"Nervous?"

"I got married today, or didn't you notice?"

"And that made you nervous?"

"Sure. Because you're afraid you made a mistake. I wasn't sure you were even going to show. I'm still not sure it actually happened."

"I thought about it, Sinj. I thought about it a lot. I barely know you. I was worried that it was only, you know—lust."

"Hmnn, there is that. Of course, I wonder what you felt when you were locked up in that hut. Only lust?"

"That's funny. It's exactly what Rosa asked me." She shook her head. She had pined for him, grieved for him. It had been love.

"And when I thought you might be dead. I guess that was because I wanted a good lay?"

"Am I a good lay?"

"Don't change the subject. What scares you, Tam? That you made a mistake? That you don't love me? That I don't love you?"

"That you only want me physically. Yes, that you don't really love me. Because, you see, how could someone like you, someone who looks like you, how could the impossibly beautiful, impossibly brilliant St. John Twaine want me for the rest of his life? I could not possibly be this lucky."

He smiled brilliantly. "That's the nicest thing anyone's ever said to me." He kissed the palm of her hand. "Tell me more about how gorgeous I am." She groaned and his grin grew broader.

"My God, Sinj, you're serious! You can't possibly be that vain. Or is it insecurity?" It dawned on her. He didn't really know, didn't really understand, deep down, how special he was. He had thrown himself into his work and hadn't come up for air in so long, he had lost his measure of himself. He needed to know he was enough as badly as she did. No, more.

"You know, Professor. I don't only love you for your incredible body and face, although it helps a hell of a lot."

"No?"

"No. Your mind drives me fucking crazy. The way you work, the way you think."

"Plus," he winked, "I took a bullet for you, don't forget that. Well, not exactly, but it sounds dramatic."

They talked about the wedding and laughed, sipping champagne. Tam finally took in a deep breath and knew it was time.

"Honey, I'll be back." She saw a brief flash of panic on his face. "To the bathroom. Geesh. Relax."

She called over her shoulder. "When I come out, I'd like you to be ready for me. Or there will be consequences."

"Oh my God," he moaned. "What consequences? Oh Tam. God help me."

She smiled at his response as she closed the door and silently thanked Cynthia for helping her to pick out her lingerie. "I think he wants a take-charge kind of outfit,"

Cynthia had said as she pointed to the outfit Tam now changed into.

When she emerged, he lay on his side, gloriously naked, cock jutting out, dark hair falling into his smoldering eyes.

"You look like a dark mistress now. I've never seen anything so sexy in my life."

"Do it now." She smiled, but her voice said business.

"And what if I don't?"

"Then you don't get what you want, Professor. And I know what you want. So do it now. Just like before. You know what it does to me. You're the biggest tease alive." She knelt near the edge of the bed as he reached for his cock and began his long strokes, his journey into bliss.

His eyes misted over. "Tell me what you want."

Tam felt her pussy throb as she watched his hand move back and forth.

"Please kiss me. I want you near me."

She leaned in and gave him a quick peck on the lips and he reached up to pull her into his arms.

"No, no, no. Not yet." Tam reached into her suitcase and drew out scarves, four of them.

"Oh my God, Tam!"

She knew it was a game. He could overpower her any second he wanted. It didn't matter, because she was giving him exactly what he wanted.

"All right, arms up." She watched him squirm as she pulled out another scarf.

She leaned in and kissed him thoroughly as he tried to pull his arms free. She blindfolded him and began her play.

"You are delicious, Professor. Simply delicious." He groaned in delight, in agony, his cock huge, throbbing in her palm. "What will you do if I make you come?"

"Anything."

"What will you do, Professor?"

"I'll eat your pussy all night. I'll fuck you until you can't take anymore. I'll let you..."

"Hmm?"

"Please, I'll take you anywhere you want to go." She ran ice on his nipples and then brought it into her mouth and moved to his cock. With just a few licks and sucks, and he erupted fiercely, crying out to her.

"God, Tam, what was that! I've never come so quickly in my life." He reached for her. "Please, come here, I have to hold you."

She took off his blindfold and kissed him.

"You are too perfect, Tam. I love you. I love you so much it's killing me. Do you understand? Untie me!" She let him go and he threw her onto the bed, ripping off her lingerie, yanking down her stockings.

Tam pushed him away and walked onto the balcony, leaned on the railing, and thrust her ass out. She called to him over her shoulder. "Professor, the action has moved outside." He was behind her in no time, rubbing her from behind, first her breasts, then her clit. She was nearly ready to come when he thrust into her. She cried out, never having felt anything fill her so deeply, so completely.

SinJin began moaning as he thrust in a slow, steady rhythm, and he whispered in her ear as he did. "I'm fucking you hard honey, so you had better hold on. Tell me you want this, tell me how much you want this. Big enough for you, wife? Deep enough, wife?"

"Sinj, oh my God." She couldn't say another word. She was undone, shattered as he picked up the pace and pounded into her, squeezing her hips so hard she knew he'd leave marks on her. The fire inside her built and built. He didn't stop talking, taunting her roughly. "Order me, Tam. And the next time, honey, we'll find something a little kinkier than silk scarves. Would that be okay?"

"That would be incredible, Professor. Teach me everything you know. Everything you've ever dreamed of." She was hoarse and began repeating his name. He bit into her neck as he came and then cried her name into the night air.

"Tell my story!"

They both heard the unearthly laugh and looked at one another.

"Who brought him on the honeymoon?" Tam laughed nervously.

SinJin shook his head in wonder and called out into the night air. "Buddy, give me one night! I'll tell your damned story, I promise!"

SinJin pulled Tam into his arms and carried her to the bed. He knelt at her side and brushed his hand along her cheek.

"Wife?"

"Yes, husband?"

"Am I enough? Forever?"

"Yes, Professor. You always were. I love you so much it hurts."

"When you walked up the path to Cozmano in that ridiculous suit, I had the oddest feeling my life was about to change. You know, Tam, now I know what the curse was. It was life without you."

SinJin closed his eyes, and Tam hugged him closely.

"What is it, Professor?"

"Just thanking Shield Jaguar."

"Tell him thanks for me, too."

☽ ☽ ☽

Shield Jaguar turned to A'ok. "And that's how I saved a young woman from death and healed her lover's heart."

"And I thought you didn't care if anyone lived or died? Some fearsome slayer you are!"

"Oh, love, you know that's not true. How about the Spanish lady with the evil husband?"

And Shield Jaguar began his second tale of the evening as they rode the Sun beneath the horizon.

Samhain Publishing, Ltd.

It's all about the story...

Action/Adventure
Fantasy
Historical
Horror
Mainstream
Mystery/Suspense
Non-Fiction
Paranormal
Red Hots!
Romance
Science Fiction
Western
Young Adult

http://www.samhainpublishing.com

Printed in the United States
71090LV00002B/106